Youth

Youth

Leo Tolstoy

MINT EDITIONS

Youth was first published in 1856.

This edition published by Mint Editions 2021.

ISBN 9781513291291 | E-ISBN 9781513294148

Published by Mint Editions®

 MINT
EDITIONS

minteditionbooks.com

Publishing Director: Jennifer Newens
Design & Production: Rachel Lopez Metzger
Project Manager: Micaela Clark
Translated by C. J. Hogarth
Typesetting: Westchester Publishing Services

Contents

I

What I Consider to Have Been the Beginning of My Youth

I have said that my friendship with Dimitri opened up for me a new view of my life and of its aim and relations. The essence of that view lay in the conviction that the destiny of man is to strive for moral improvement, and that such improvement is at once easy, possible, and lasting. Hitherto, however, I had found pleasure only in the new ideas which I discovered to arise from that conviction, and in the forming of brilliant plans for a moral, active future, while all the time my life had been continuing along its old petty, muddled, pleasure-seeking course, and the same virtuous thoughts which I and my adored friend Dimitri ("my own marvellous Mitia," as I used to call him to myself in a whisper) had been wont to exchange with one another still pleased my intellect, but left my sensibility untouched. Nevertheless there came a moment when those thoughts swept into my head with a sudden freshness and force of moral revelation which left me aghast at the amount of time which I had been wasting, and made me feel as though I must at once—that very second—apply those thoughts to life, with the firm intention of never again changing them.

It is from that moment that I date the beginning of my youth.

I was then nearly sixteen. Tutors still attended to give me lessons, St. Jerome still acted as general supervisor of my education, and, willy-nilly, I was being prepared for the University. In addition to my studies, my occupations included certain vague dreamings and ponderings, a number of gymnastic exercises to make myself the finest athlete in the world, a good deal of aimless, thoughtless wandering through the rooms of the house (but more especially along the maidservants' corridor), and much looking at myself in the mirror. From the latter, however, I always turned away with a vague feeling of depression, almost of repulsion. Not only did I feel sure that my exterior was ugly, but I could derive no comfort from any of the usual consolations under such circumstances. I could not say, for instance, that I had at least an expressive, clever, or refined face, for there was nothing whatever expressive about it. Its features were of the most humdrum, dull, and unbecoming type, with small grey eyes which seemed to me, whenever I regarded them in the mirror, to be stupid rather than clever. Of manly bearing I possessed even less, since, although I was not exactly small of stature, and had, moreover, plenty of strength for my years, every feature in my face was of the meek, sleepy-looking, indefinite type. Even refinement was lacking in it, since, on the contrary, it precisely resembled that of a simple-looking moujik, while I also had the same big hands and feet as he. At the time, all this seemed to me very shameful.

II

Springtime

Easter of the year when I entered the University fell late in April, so that the examinations were fixed for St. Thomas's Week, (Easter week.) and I had to spend Good Friday in fasting and finally getting myself ready for the ordeal.

Following upon wet snow (the kind of stuff which Karl Ivanitch used to describe as "a child following, its father"), the weather had for three days been bright and mild and still. Not a clot of snow was now to be seen in the streets, and the dirty slush had given place to wet, shining pavements and coursing rivulets. The last icicles on the roofs were fast melting in the sunshine, buds were swelling on the trees in the little garden, the path leading across the courtyard to the stables was soft instead of being a frozen ridge of mud, and mossy grass was showing green between the stones around the entrance-steps. It was just that particular time in spring when the season exercises the strongest influence upon the human soul—when clear sunlight illuminates everything, yet sheds no warmth, when rivulets run trickling under one's feet, when the air is charged with an odorous freshness, and when the bright blue sky is streaked with long, transparent clouds.

For some reason or another the influence of this early stage in the birth of spring always seems to me more perceptible and more impressive in a great town than in the country. One sees less, but one feels more. I was standing near the window—through the double frames of which the morning sun was throwing its mote-flecked beams upon the floor of what seemed to me my intolerably wearisome schoolroom—and working out a long algebraical equation on the blackboard. In one hand I was holding a ragged, long-suffering "Algebra" and in the other a small piece of chalk which had already besmeared my hands, my face, and the elbows of my jacket. Nicola, clad in an apron, and with his sleeves rolled up, was picking out the putty from the window-frames with a pair of nippers, and unfastening the screws. The window looked out upon the little garden. At length his occupation and the noise which he was making over it arrested my attention. At the moment I was in a very cross, dissatisfied frame of mind, for nothing seemed to be going right with me. I had made a mistake at the very beginning of my algebra, and so should have to work it out again; twice I had let the chalk drop. I was conscious that my hands and face were whitened all over; the sponge had rolled away into a corner; and the noise of Nicola's operations was fast getting on my nerves. I had a feeling as though I wanted to fly into a temper and grumble at some one, so I threw down chalk and "Algebra" alike, and began to pace the room. Then suddenly I remembered that today we were to go to confession, and that therefore I must refrain from doing anything wrong. Next, with equal suddenness I relapsed into an extraordinarily goodhumoured frame of mind, and walked across to Nicola.

"Let me help you, Nicola," I said, trying to speak as pleasantly as I possibly could. The idea that I was performing a meritorious action in thus suppressing my ill-temper and offering to help him increased my good-humour all the more.

By this time the putty had been chipped out, and the screws removed, yet, though Nicola pulled with might and main at the cross-piece, the window-frame refused to budge.

"If it comes out as soon as he and I begin to pull at it together," I thought, "it will be rather a shame, as then I shall have nothing more of the kind to do today."

Suddenly the frame yielded a little at one side, and came out.

"Where shall I put it?" I said.

"Let ME see to it, if you please," replied Nicola, evidently surprised as well as, seemingly, not over-pleased at my zeal. "We must not leave it here, but carry it away to the lumber-room, where I keep all the frames stored and numbered."

"Oh, but I can manage it," I said as I lifted it up. I verily believe that if the lumber-room had been a couple of versts away, and the frame twice as heavy as it was, I should have been the more pleased. I felt as though I wanted to tire myself out in performing this service for Nicola. When I returned to the room the bricks and screws had been replaced on the windowsill, and Nicola was sweeping the debris, as well as a few torpid flies, out of the open window. The fresh, fragrant air was rushing into and filling all the room, while with it came also the dull murmur of the city and the twittering of sparrows in the garden. Everything was in brilliant light, the room looked cheerful, and a gentle spring breeze was stirring Nicola's hair and the leaves of my "Algebra." Approaching the window, I sat down upon the sill, turned my eyes downwards towards the garden, and fell into a brown study.

Something new to me, something extraordinarily potent and unfamiliar, had suddenly invaded my soul. The wet ground on which, here and there, a few yellowish stalks and blades of bright-green grass were to be seen; the little rivulets glittering in the sunshine, and sweeping clods of earth and tiny chips of wood along with them; the reddish twigs of the lilac, with their swelling buds, which nodded just beneath the window; the fussy twitterings of birds as they fluttered in the bush below; the blackened fence shining wet from the snow which had lately melted off it; and, most of all, the raw, odorous air and radiant sunlight—all spoke to me, clearly and unmistakably, of something new and beautiful, of something which, though I cannot repeat it here as it was then expressed to me, I will try to reproduce so far as I understood it. Everything spoke to me of beauty, happiness, and virtue—as three things which were both easy and possible for me—and said that no one of them could exist without the other two, since beauty, happiness, and virtue were one. "How did I never come to understand that before?" I cried to myself. "How did I ever manage to be so wicked? Oh, but how good, how happy, I could be—nay, I WILL be—in the future! At once, at once—yes, this very minute—I will become another being, and begin to live differently!" For all that, I continued sitting on the window-sill, continued merely dreaming, and doing nothing. Have you ever, on a summer's day, gone to bed in dull, rainy weather, and, waking just at sunset, opened your eyes and seen through the square space of the window—the space where the linen blind is blowing up and down, and beating its rod upon the window-sill—the rain-soaked, shadowy, purple vista of an avenue of lime-trees, with a damp garden path lit up by the clear, slanting beams of the sun, and then suddenly heard the joyous sounds of bird life in the garden, and seen insects flying to and fro at the open window, and glittering in the sunlight, and smelt the fragrance of the rain-washed air, and thought to yourself, "Am I not ashamed to be lying in bed on such an evening as this?" and, leaping joyously to your feet, gone out into the garden and revelled in all that welter of life? If you have, then you can imagine for yourself the overpowering sensation which was then possessing me.

III

Dreams

"Today I will make my confession and purge myself of every sin," I thought to myself. "Nor will I ever commit another one." At this point I recalled all the peccadilloes which most troubled my conscience. "I will go to church regularly every Sunday, as well as read the Gospel at the close of every hour throughout the day. What is more, I will set aside, out of the cheque which I shall receive each month after I have gone to the University, two-and-a-half roubles" (a tenth of my monthly allowance) "for people who are poor but not exactly beggars, yet without letting any one know anything about it. Yes, I will begin to look out for people like that—orphans or old women—at once, yet never tell a soul what I am doing for them.

"Also, I will have a room here of my very own (St. Jerome's, probably), and look after it myself, and keep it perfectly clean. I will never let any one do anything for me, for every one is just a human being like myself. Likewise I will walk every day, not drive, to the University. Even if some one gives me a drozhki (Russian phaeton.) I will sell it, and devote the money to the poor. Everything I will do exactly and always" (what that "always" meant I could not possibly have said, but at least I had a vivid consciousness of its connoting some kind of prudent, moral, and irreproachable life). "I will get up all my lectures thoroughly, and go over all the subjects beforehand, so that at the end of my first course I may come out top and write a thesis. During my second course also I will get up everything beforehand, so that I may soon be transferred to the third course, and at eighteen come out top in the examinations, and receive two gold medals, and go on to be Master of Arts, and Doctor, and the first scholar in Europe. Yes, in all Europe I mean to be the first scholar.—Well, what next?" I asked myself at this point. Suddenly it struck me that dreams of this sort were a form of pride—a sin which I should have to confess to the priest that very evening, so I returned to the original thread of my meditations. "When getting up my lectures I will go to the Vorobievi Gori, (Sparrow Hills—a public park near Moscow.) and choose some spot under a tree, and read my lectures over there. Sometimes I will take with me something to eat—cheese or a pie from Pedotti's, or something of the kind. After that I will sleep a little, and then read some good book or other, or else draw pictures or play on some instrument (certainly I must learn to play the flute). Perhaps SHE too will be walking on the Vorobievi Gori, and will approach me one day and say, 'Who are you?' and I shall look at her, oh, so sadly, and say that I am the son of a priest, and that I am happy only when I am there alone, quite alone. Then she will give me her hand, and say something to me, and sit down beside me. So every day we shall go to the same spot, and be friends together, and I shall kiss her. But no! That would not be right! On the contrary, from this day forward I never mean to look at a woman again. Never, never again do I mean to walk with a girl, nor even to go near one if I can help it. Yet, of course, in three years' time, when I have come of age, I shall marry. Also, I mean to take as much exercise as ever I can, and to do gymnastics every day, so that, when I have turned twenty-five, I shall be stronger even than Rappo. On my first day's training I mean to hold out half a pood (The Pood = 40 Russian pounds.) at arm's length for five minutes, and the next day twenty-one pounds, and the third day twenty-two pounds, and so on, until at last I can hold out four poods in each hand, and be stronger even than a porter. Then, if ever any one should try to insult me or should begin to speak disrespectfully of HER, I shall take him so, by the front of his coat, and lift him up an arshin (The arshin = 2 feet 3 inches.) or two with one hand, and just hold him there, so that he may feel my strength and cease from his conduct. Yet that too would not be right. No, no, it would not matter; I should not hurt him, merely show him that I—"

Let no one blame me because the dreams of my youth were as foolish as those of my childhood and boyhood. I am sure that, even if it be my fate to live to extreme old age and to continue my story with the years, I, an old man of seventy, shall be found dreaming dreams just as impossible and childish as those I am dreaming now. I shall be dreaming of some lovely Maria who loves me, the toothless old man, as she might love a Mazeppa; of some imbecile son who, through some extraordinary chance, has suddenly become a minister of state; of my suddenly receiving a windfall of a million of roubles. I am sure that there exists no human being, no human age, to whom or to which that gracious, consolatory power of dreaming is totally a stranger. Yet, save for the one general feature of magic and impossibility, the dreams of each human being, of each age of man, have their own distinguishing characteristics. At the period upon which I look as having marked the close of my boyhood and the beginning of my youth, four leading sentiments formed the basis of my dreams. The first of those sentiments was love for HER—for an imaginary woman whom I always pictured the same in my dreams, and whom I somehow expected to meet some day and somewhere. This she of mine had a little of Sonetchka in her, a little of Masha as Masha could look when she stood washing linen over the clothes-tub, and a little of a certain woman with pearls round her fair white neck whom I had once seen long, long ago at a theatre, in a box below our own. My second sentiment was a craving for love. I wanted every one to know me and to love me. I wanted to be able to utter my name—Nicola Irtenieff—and at once to see every one thunderstruck at it, and come crowding round me and thanking me for something or another, I hardly knew what. My third sentiment was the expectation of some extraordinary, glorious happiness that was impending—some happiness so strong and assured as to verge upon ecstasy. Indeed, so firmly persuaded was I that very, very soon some unexpected chance would suddenly make me the richest and most famous man in the world that I lived in constant, tremulous expectation of this magic good fortune befalling me. I was always thinking to myself that "IT is beginning," and that I should go on thereafter to attain everything that a man could wish for. Consequently, I was for ever hurrying from place to place, in the belief that "IT" must be "beginning" just where I happened not to be. Lastly, my fourth and principal sentiment of all was abhorrence of myself, mingled with regret—yet a regret so blended with the certain expectation of happiness to which I have referred that it had in it nothing of sorrow. It seemed to me that it would be so easy and natural for me to tear myself away from my past and to remake it—to forget all that had been, and to begin my life, with all its relations, anew—that the past never troubled me, never clung to me at all. I even found a certain pleasure in detesting the past, and in seeing it in a darker light than the true one. This note of regret and of a curious longing for perfection were the chief mental impressions which I gathered from that new stage of my growth—impressions which imparted new principles to my view of myself, of men, and of God's world. O good and consoling voice, which in later days, in sorrowful days when my soul yielded silently to the sway of life's falseness and depravity, so often raised a sudden, bold protest against all iniquity, as well as mercilessly exposed the past, commanded, nay, compelled, me to love only the pure vista of the present, and promised me all that was fair and happy in the future! O good and consoling voice! Surely the day will never come when you are silent?

IV

OUR FAMILY CIRCLE

Papa was seldom at home that spring. Yet, whenever he was so, he seemed extraordinarily cheerful as he either strummed his favourite pieces on the piano or looked roguishly at us and made jokes about us all, not excluding even Mimi. For instance, he would say that the Tsarevitch himself had seen Mimi at the rink, and fallen so much in love with her that he had presented a petition to the Synod for divorce; or else that I had been granted an appointment as secretary to the Austrian ambassador—a piece of news which he imparted to us with a perfectly grave face. Next, he would frighten Katenka with some spiders (of which she was very much afraid), engage in an animated conversation with our friends Dubkoff and Nechludoff, and tell us and our guests, over and over again, his plans for the year. Although these plans changed almost from day to day, and were for ever contradicting one another, they seemed so attractive that we were always glad to listen to them, and Lubotshka, in particular, would glue her eyes to his face, so as not to lose a single word. One day his plan would be that he should leave my brother and myself at the University, and go and live with Lubotshka in Italy for two years. Next, the plan would be that he should buy an estate on the south coast of the Crimea, and take us for an annual visit there; next, that we should migrate en masse to St. Petersburg; and so forth. Yet, in addition to this unusual cheerfulness of his, another change had come over him of late—a change which greatly surprised me. This was that he had had some fashionable clothes made—an olive-coloured frockcoat, smart trousers with straps at the sides, and a long wadded greatcoat which fitted him to perfection. Often, too, there was a delightful smell of scent about him when he came home from a party—more especially when he had been to see a lady of whom Mimi never spoke but with a sigh and a face that seemed to say: "Poor orphans! How dreadful! It is a good thing that SHE is gone now!" and so on, and so on. From Nicola (for Papa never spoke to us of his gambling) I had learnt that he (Papa) had been very fortunate in play that winter, and so had won an extraordinary amount of money, all of which he had placed in the bank after vowing that he would play no more that spring. Evidently, it was his fear of being unable to resist again doing so that was rendering him anxious to leave for the country as soon as possible. Indeed, he ended by deciding not to wait until I had entered the University, but to take the girls to Petrovskoe immediately after Easter, and to leave Woloda and myself to follow them at a later season.

All that winter, until the opening of spring, Woloda had been inseparable from Dubkoff, while at the same time the pair of them had cooled greatly towards Dimitri. Their chief amusements (so I gathered from conversations overheard) were continual drinking of champagne, sledge-driving past the windows of a lady with whom both of them appeared to be in love, and dancing with her—not at children's parties, either, but at real balls! It was this last fact which, despite our love for one another, placed a vast gulf between Woloda and myself. We felt that the distance between a boy still taking lessons under a tutor and a man who danced at real, grown-up balls was too great to allow of their exchanging mutual ideas. Katenka, too, seemed grown-up now, and read innumerable novels; so that the idea that she would some day be getting married no longer seemed to me a joke. Yet, though she and Woloda were thus grown-up, they never made friends with one another, but, on the contrary, seemed to cherish a mutual contempt. In general, when Katenka was at home alone, nothing but novels amused her, and they but slightly; but as soon as ever a visitor of the opposite sex called, she at once grew lively and amiable, and used her eyes for saying things which I could not then understand. It was only later, when she one day informed me in conversation that the only thing a girl was allowed to indulge in was coquetry—coquetry of the eyes, I mean—that I understood those strange contortions of her features which to every one else had seemed a matter for no surprise at all. Lubotshka also had begun to wear what was almost a long dress—a dress which almost concealed her goose-shaped feet; yet she still remained as ready a weeper as ever. She dreamed now of marrying, not a hussar, but a singer or an instrumentalist, and accordingly applied herself to her music with greater diligence than ever. St. Jerome, who knew that he was going to remain with us only until my examinations were over, and so had obtained for himself a new post in the family of some count or another, now looked with contempt upon the members of our household. He stayed indoors very little, took to smoking cigarettes (then all the rage), and was for ever whistling lively tunes on the edge of a card. Mimi daily grew more and more despondent, as though, now that we were beginning to grow up, she looked for nothing good from any one or anything.

When, on the day of which I am speaking, I went in to luncheon I found only Mimi, Katenka, Lubotshka, and St. Jerome in the dining-room. Papa was away, and Woloda in his own room, doing some preparation work for his examinations in company with a party of his comrades: wherefore he had requested that lunch should be sent to him there. Of late, Mimi had usually taken the head of the table, and as none of us had any respect for her, luncheon had lost most of its refinement and charm. That is to say, the meal was no longer what it had been in Mamma's or our grandmother's time, namely, a kind of rite which brought all the family together at a given hour and divided the day into two halves. We allowed ourselves to come in as late as the second course, to drink wine in tumblers (St. Jerome himself set us the example), to roll about on our chairs, to depart without saying grace, and so on. In fact, luncheon had ceased to be a family ceremony. In the old days at Petrovskoe, every one had been used to wash and dress for the meal, and then to repair to the drawing-room as the appointed hour (two o'clock) drew near, and pass the time of waiting in lively conversation. Just as the clock in the servants' hall was beginning to whirr before striking the hour, Foka would enter with noiseless footsteps, and, throwing his napkin over his arm and assuming a dignified, rather severe expression, would say in loud, measured tones: "Luncheon is ready!" Thereupon, with pleased, cheerful faces, we would form a procession—the elders going first and the juniors following, and, with much rustling of starched petticoats and subdued creaking of boots and shoes—would proceed to the dining-room, where, still talking in undertones, the company would seat themselves in their accustomed places. Or, again, at Moscow, we would all of us be standing before the table ready-laid in the hall, talking quietly among ourselves as we waited for our grandmother, whom the butler, Gabriel, had gone to acquaint with the fact that luncheon was ready. Suddenly the door would open, there would come the faint swish of a dress and the sound of footsteps, and our grandmother—dressed in a mob-cap trimmed with a quaint old lilac bow, and wearing either a smile or a severe expression on her face according as the state of her health inclined her—would issue from her room. Gabriel would hasten to precede her to her arm-chair, the other chairs would make a scraping sound, and, with a feeling as though a cold shiver (the precursor of appetite) were running down one's back, one would seize upon one's damp, starched napkin, nibble a morsel or two of bread, and, rubbing one's hands softly under the table, gaze with eager, radiant impatience at the steaming plates of soup which the butler was beginning to dispense in order of ranks and ages or according to the favour of our grandmother.

On the present occasion, however, I was conscious of neither excitement nor pleasure when I went in to luncheon. Even the mingled chatter of Mimi, the girls, and St. Jerome about the horrible boots of our Russian tutor, the pleated dresses worn by the young Princesses Kornakoff, and so forth (chatter which at any other time would have filled me with a sincerity of contempt which I should have been at no pains to conceal—at all events so far as Lubotshka and Katenka were concerned), failed to shake the benevolent frame of mind into which I had fallen. I was unusually good humoured that day, and listened to everything with a smile and a studied air of kindness. Even when I asked for the kvas I did so politely, while I lost not a moment in agreeing with St. Jerome when he told me that it was undoubtedly more correct to say "Je peux" than "Je puis." Yet, I must confess to a certain disappointment at finding that no one paid any particular attention to my politeness and good-humour. After luncheon, Lubotshka showed me a paper on which she had written down a list of her sins: upon which I observed that, although the idea was excellent so far as it went, it would be still better for her to write down her sins on her SOUL—"a very different matter."

"Why is it 'a very different matter'?" asked Lubotshka.

"Never mind: that is all right; you do not understand me," and I went upstairs to my room, telling St. Jerome that I was going to work, but in reality purposing to occupy the hour and a half before confession time in writing down a list of my daily tasks and duties which should last me all my life, together with a statement of my life's aim, and the rules by which I meant unswervingly to be guided.

V

My Rules

I took some sheets of paper, and tried, first of all, to make a list of my tasks and duties for the coming year. The paper needed ruling, but, as I could not find the ruler, I had to use a Latin dictionary instead. The result was that, when I had drawn the pen along the edge of the dictionary and removed the latter, I found that, in place of a line, I had only made an oblong smudge on the paper, since the dictionary was not long enough to reach across it, and the pen had slipped round the soft, yielding corner of the book. Thereupon I took another piece of paper, and, by carefully manipulating the dictionary, contrived to rule what at least RESEMBLED lines. Dividing my duties into three sections—my duties to myself, my duties to my neighbour, and my duties to God—I started to indite a list of the first of those sections, but they seemed to me so numerous, and therefore requiring to be divided into so many species and subdivisions, that I thought I had better first of all write down the heading of "Rules of My Life" before proceeding to their detailed inscription. Accordingly, I proceeded to write "Rules of My Life" on the outside of the six sheets of paper which I had made into a sort of folio, but the words came out in such a crooked and uneven scrawl that for long I sat debating the question, "Shall I write them again?"—for long, sat in agonised contemplation of the ragged handwriting and disfigured title-page. Why was it that all the beauty and clarity which my soul then contained came out so misshapenly on paper (as in life itself) just when I was wishing to apply those qualities to what I was thinking at the moment?

"The priest is here, so please come downstairs and hear his directions," said Nicola as he entered.

Hurriedly concealing my folio under the table-cloth, I looked at myself in the mirror, combed my hair upwards (I imagined this to give me a pensive air), and descended to the divannaia, (Room with divans, or ante-room) where the table stood covered with a cloth and had an ikon and candles placed upon it. Papa entered just as I did, but by another door: whereupon the priest—a grey-headed old monk with a severe, elderly face—blessed him, and Papa kissed his small, squat, wizened hand. I did the same.

"Go and call Woldemar," said Papa. "Where is he? Wait a minute, though. Perhaps he is preparing for the Communion at the University?"

"No, he is with the Prince," said Katenka, and glanced at Lubotshka. Suddenly the latter blushed for some reason or another, and then frowned. Finally, pretending that she was not well, she left the room, and I followed her. In the drawing-room she halted, and began to pencil something fresh on her paper of peccadilloes.

"Well, what new sin have you gone and committed?" I asked.

"Nothing," she replied with another blush. All at once we heard Dimitri's voice raised in the hall as he took his leave of Woloda.

"It seems to me you are always experiencing some new temptation," said Katenka, who had entered the room behind us, and now stood looking at Lubotshka.

What was the matter with my sister I could not conceive, but she was now so agitated that the tears were starting from her eyes. Finally her confusion grew uncontrollable, and vented itself in rage against both herself and Katenka, who appeared to be teasing her.

"Any one can see that you are a FOREIGNER!" she cried (nothing offended Katenka so much as to be called by that term, which is why Lubotshka used it). "Just because I have the secret of which you know," she went on, with anger ringing through her tone, "you purposely go and upset me! Please do understand that it is no joking matter."

"Do you know what she has gone and written on her paper, Nicolinka?" cried Katenka, much infuriated by the term "foreigner." "She has written down that—"

"Oh, I never could have believed that you could be so cruel!" exclaimed Lubotshka, now bursting into open sobbing as she moved away from us. "You chose that moment on purpose! You spend your whole time in trying to make me sin! I'll never go to You again for sympathy and advice!"

VI

Confession

With these and other disjointed impressions in my mind, I returned to the divannaia. As soon as every one had reassembled, the priest rose and prepared to read the prayer before confession. The instant that the silence was broken by the stern, expressive voice of the monk as he recited the prayer—and more especially when he addressed to us the words: "Reveal thou all thy sins without shame, concealment, or extenuation, and let thy soul be cleansed before God: for if thou concealest aught, then great will be thy sin"—the same sensation of reverent awe came over me as I had felt during the morning. I even took a certain pleasure in recognising this condition of mine, and strove to preserve it, not only by restraining all other thoughts from entering my brain, but also by consciously exerting myself to feel no other sensation than this same one of reverence.

Papa was the first to go to confession. He remained a long, long time in the room which had belonged to our grandmother, and during that time the rest of us kept silence in the divannaia, or only whispered to one another on the subject of who should precede whom. At length, the voice of the priest again reading the prayer sounded from the doorway, and then Papa's footsteps. The door creaked as he came out, coughing and holding one shoulder higher than the other, in his usual way, and for the moment he did not look at any of us.

"You go now, Luba," he said presently, as he gave her cheek a mischievous pinch. "Mind you tell him everything. You are my greatest sinner, you know."

Lubotshka went red and pale by turns, took her memorandum paper out of her apron, replaced it, and finally moved away towards the doorway with her head sunk between her shoulders as though she expected to receive a blow upon it from above. She was not long gone, and when she returned her shoulders were shaking with sobs.

At length—next after the excellent Katenka (who came out of the doorway with a smile on her face)—my turn arrived. I entered the dimly-lighted room with the same vague feeling of awe, the same conscious eagerness to arouse that feeling more and more in my soul, that had possessed me up to the present moment. The priest, standing in front of a reading-desk, slowly turned his face to me.

I was not more than five minutes in the room, but came out from it happy and (so I persuaded myself) entirely cleansed—a new, a morally reborn individual. Despite the fact that the old surroundings of my life now struck me as unfamiliar (even though the rooms, the furniture, and my own figure—would to heavens that I could have changed my outer man for the better in the same way that I believed myself to have changed my inner I—were the same as before), I remained in that comfortable attitude of mine until the very moment of bedtime.

Yet, no sooner had I begun to grow drowsy with the conning over of my sins than in a flash I recollected a particularly shameful sin which I had suppressed at confession time. Instantly the words of the prayer before confession came back to my memory and began sounding in my ears. My peace was gone for ever. "For if thou concealest aught, then great will be thy sin." Each time that the phrase recurred to me I saw myself a sinner for whom no punishment was adequate. Long did I toss from side to side as I considered my position, while expecting every moment to be visited with the divine wrath—to be struck with sudden death, perhaps!—an insupportable thought! Then suddenly the reassuring thought occurred to me: "Why should I not drive out to the monastery when the morning comes, and see the priest again, and make a second confession?" Thereafter I grew calmer.

VII

The Expedition to the Monastery

S everal times that night I woke in terror at the thought that I might be oversleeping myself, and by six o'clock was out of bed, although the dawn was hardly peeping in at the window. I put on my clothes and boots (all of which were lying tumbled and unbrushed beside the bed, since Nicola, of course had not been in yet to tidy them up), and, without a prayer said or my face washed, emerged, for the first time in my life, into the street ALONE.

Over the way, behind the green roof of a large building, the dim, cold dawn was beginning to blush red. The keen frost of the spring morning which had stiffened the pools and mud and made them crackle under my feet now nipped my face and hands also. Not a cab was to be seen, though I had counted upon one to make the journey out and home the quicker. Only a file of waggons was rumbling along the Arbat Prospect, and a couple of bricklayers talking noisily together as they strode along the pavement. However, after walking a verst or so I began to meet men and women taking baskets to market or going with empty barrels to fetch the day's water supply; until at length, at the cross streets near the Arbat Gate, where a pieman had set up his stall and a baker was just opening his shop, I espied an old cabman shaking himself after indulging in a nap on the box of his be-scratched old blue-painted, hobble-de-hoy wreck of a drozhki. He seemed barely awake as he asked twenty copecks as the fare to the monastery and back, but came to himself a moment afterwards, just as I was about to get in, and, touching up his horse with the spare end of the reins, started to drive off and leave me. "My horse wants feeding," he growled, "I can't take you, barin. (Sir)"

With some difficulty and a promise of FORTY copecks I persuaded him to stop. He eyed me narrowly as he pulled up, but nevertheless said: "Very well. Get in, barin." I must confess that I had some qualms lest he should drive me to a quiet corner somewhere, and then rob me, but I caught hold of the collar of his ragged driving-coat, close to where his wrinkled neck showed sadly lean above his hunched-up back, and climbed on to the blue-painted, curved, rickety scat. As we set off along

LEO TOLSTOY

Vozdvizhenka Street, I noticed that the back of the drozhki was covered with a strip of the same greenish material as that of which his coat was made. For some reason or another this reassured me, and I no longer felt nervous of being taken to a quiet spot and robbed.

The sun had risen to a good height, and was gilding the cupolas of the churches, when we arrived at the monastery. In the shade the frost had not yet given, but in the open roadway muddy rivulets of water were coursing along, and it was through fast-thawing mire that the horse went clip-clopping his way. Alighting, and entering the monastery grounds, I inquired of the first monk whom I met where I could find the priest whom I was seeking.

"His cell is over there," replied the monk as he stopped a moment and pointed towards a little building up to which a flight of steps led.

"I respectfully thank you," I said, and then fell to wondering what all the monks (who at that moment began to come filing out of the church) must be thinking of me as they glanced in my direction. I was neither a grown-up nor a child, while my face was unwashed, my hair unbrushed, my clothes tumbled, and my boots unblacked and muddy. To what class of persons were the brethren assigning me—for they stared at me hard enough? Nevertheless I proceeded in the direction which the young priest had pointed out to me.

An old man with bushy grey eyebrows and a black cassock met me on the narrow path to the cells, and asked me what I wanted. For a brief moment I felt inclined to say "Nothing," and then run back to the drozhki and drive away home; but, for all its beetling brows, the face of the old man inspired confidence, and I merely said that I wished to see the priest (whom I named).

"Very well, young sir; I will take you to him," said the old man as he turned round. Clearly he had guessed my errand at a stroke. "The father is at matins at this moment, but he will soon be back," and, opening a door, the old man led me through a neat hall and corridor, all lined with clean matting, to a cell.

"Please to wait here," he added, and then, with a kind, reassuring glance, departed.

The little room in which I found myself was of the smallest possible dimensions, but extremely neat and clean. Its furniture only consisted of a small table (covered with a cloth, and placed between two equally small casement-windows, in which stood two pots of geraniums), a stand of ikons, with a lamp suspended in front of them, a bench, and two chairs. In one corner hung a wall clock, with little flowers painted on its dial, and brass weights to its chains, while upon two nails driven into a screen (which, fastened to the ceiling with whitewashed pegs, probably concealed the bed) hung a couple of cassocks. The windows looked out upon a whitewashed wall, about two arshins distant, and in the space between them there grew a small lilac-bush.

Not a sound penetrated from without, and in the stillness the measured, friendly stroke of the clock's pendulum seemed to beat quite loudly. The instant that I found myself alone in this calm retreat all other thoughts and recollections left my head as completely as though they had never been there, and I subsided into an inexpressibly pleasing kind of torpor. The rusty alpaca cassocks with their frayed linings, the worn black leather bindings of the books with their metal clasps, the dull-green plants with their carefully watered leaves and soil, and, above all, the abrupt, regular beat of the pendulum, all spoke to me intimately of some new life hitherto unknown to me—a life of unity and prayer, of calm, restful happiness.

"The months, the years, may pass," I thought to myself, "but he remains alone—always at peace, always knowing that his conscience is pure before God, that his prayer will be heard by Him." For fully half an hour I sat on that chair, trying not to move, not even to breathe loudly, for fear I should mar the harmony of the sounds which were telling me so much, and ever the pendulum continued to beat the same—now a little louder to the right, now a little softer to the left.

VIII

The Second Confession

Suddenly the sound of the priest's footsteps roused me from this reverie.

"Good morning to you," he said as he smoothed his grey hair with his hand. "What can I do for you?"

I besought him to give me his blessing, and then kissed his small, wizened hand with great fervour. After I had explained to him my errand he said nothing, but moved away towards the ikons, and began to read the exhortation: whereupon I overcame my shame, and told him all that was in my heart. Finally he laid his hands upon my head, and pronounced in his even, resonant voice the words: "My son, may the blessing of Our Heavenly Father be upon thee, and may He always preserve thee in faithfulness, loving-kindness, and meekness. Amen."

I was entirely happy. Tears of joy coursed down my face as I kissed the hem of his cassock and then raised my head again. The face of the priest expressed perfect tranquillity. So keenly did I feel the joy of reconciliation that, fearing in any way to dispel it, I took hasty leave of him, and, without looking to one side of me or the other (in order that my attention might not be distracted), left the grounds and re-entered the rickety, battered drozhki. Yet the joltings of the vehicle and the variety of objects which flitted past my eyes soon dissipated that feeling, and I became filled with nothing but the idea that the priest must have thought me the finest-spirited young man he had ever met, or ever would meet, in the whole of his life. Indeed, I reflected, there could not be many such as myself—of that I felt sure, and the conviction produced in me the kind of complacency which craves for self-communication to another. I had a great desire to unbosom myself to some one, and as there was no one else to speak to, I addressed myself to the cabman.

"Was I very long gone?" I asked him.

"No, not very long," he replied. He seemed to have grown more cheerful under the influence of the sunshine. "Yet now it is a good while past my horse's feeding-time. You see, I am a night cabman."

"Well, I only seemed to myself to be about a minute," I went on. "Do you know what I went there for?" I added, changing my seat to the well of the drozhki, so as to be nearer the driver.

"What business is it of mine? I drive a fare where he tells me to go," he replied.

"Yes, but, all the same, what do you think I went there for?" I persisted.

"I expect some one you know is going to be buried there, so you went to see about a plot for the grave."

"No, no, my friend. Still, Do you know what I went there for?"

"No, of course I cannot tell, barin," he repeated.

His voice seemed to me so kind that I decided to edify him by relating the cause of my expedition, and even telling him of the feeling which I had experienced.

"Shall I tell you?" I said. "Well, you see,"—and I told him all, as well as inflicted upon him a description of my fine sentiments. To this day I blush at the recollection.

"Well, well!" said the cabman non-committally, and for a long while afterwards he remained silent and motionless, except that at intervals he adjusted the skirt of his coat each time that it was jerked from beneath his leg by the joltings of his huge boot on the drozhki's step. I felt sure that he must be thinking of me even as the priest had done. That is to say, that he must be thinking that no such fine-spirited young man existed in the world as I. Suddenly he shot at me:

"I tell you what, barin. You ought to keep God's affairs to yourself."

"What?" I said.

"Those affairs of yours—they are God's business," he repeated, mumbling the words with his toothless lips.

"No, he has not understood me," I thought to myself, and said no more to him till we reached home.

Although it was not my original sense of reconciliation and reverence, but only a sort of complacency at having experienced such a sense, that lasted in me during the drive home (and that, too, despite the distraction of the crowds of people who now thronged the sunlit streets in every direction), I had no sooner reached home than even my spurious complacency was shattered, for I found that I had not the forty copecks wherewith to pay the cabman! To the butler, Gabriel, I already owed a small debt, and he refused to lend me any more. Seeing me twice run across the courtyard in quest of the money, the cabman must have divined the reason, for, leaping from his drozhki, he—notwithstanding that he had seemed so kind—began to bawl aloud (with an evident desire to punch my head) that people who do not pay for their cab-rides are swindlers.

None of my family were yet out of bed, so that, except for the servants, there was no one from whom to borrow the forty copecks. At length, on my most sacred, sacred word of honour to repay (a word to which, as I could see from his face, he did not altogether trust), Basil so far yielded to his fondness for me and his remembrance of the many services I had done him as to pay the cabman. Thus all my beautiful feelings ended in smoke. When I went upstairs to dress for church and go to Communion with the rest I found that my new clothes had not yet come home, and so I could not wear them. Then I sinned headlong. Donning my other suit, I went to Communion in a sad state of mental perturbation, and filled with complete distrust of all my finer impulses.

IX

How I Prepared Myself
for the Examinations

On the Thursday in Easter week Papa, my sister, Katenka, and Mimi went away into the country, and no one remained in my grandmother's great house but Woloda, St. Jerome, and myself. The frame of mind which I had experienced on the day of my confession and during my subsequent expedition to the monastery had now completely passed away, and left behind it only a dim, though pleasing, memory which daily became more and more submerged by the impressions of this emancipated existence.

The folio endorsed "Rules of My Life" lay concealed beneath a pile of school-books. Although the idea of the possibility of framing rules, for every occasion in my life and always letting myself be guided by them still pleased me (since it appeared an idea at once simple and magnificent, and I was determined to make practical application of it), I seemed somehow to have forgotten to put it into practice at once, and kept deferring doing so until such and such a moment. At the same time, I took pleasure in the thought that every idea which now entered my head could be allotted precisely to one or other of my three sections of tasks and duties—those for or to God, those for or to my neighbour, and those for or to myself. "I can always refer everything to them," I said to myself, "as well as the many, many other ideas which occur to me on one subject or another." Yet at this period I often asked myself, "Was I better and more truthful when I only believed in the power of the human intellect, or am I more so now, when I am losing the faculty of developing that power, and am in doubt both as to its potency and as to its importance?" To this I could return no positive answer.

The sense of freedom, combined with the spring-like feeling of vague expectation to which I have referred already, so unsettled me that I could not keep myself in hand—could make none but the sorriest of preparations for my University ordeal. Thus I was busy in the schoolroom one morning, and fully aware that I must work hard, seeing that tomorrow was the day of my examination in a subject of which I had the two whole questions still to read up; yet no sooner had a breath of spring come wafted through the window than I felt as though there were something quite different that I wished to recall to my memory. My hands laid down my book, my feet began to move of themselves, and to set me walking up and down the room, and my head felt as though some one had suddenly touched in it a little spring and set some machine in motion—so easily and swiftly and naturally did all sorts of pleasing fancies of which I could catch no more than the radiancy begin coursing through it. Thus one hour, two hours, elapsed unperceived. Even if I sat down determinedly to my book, and managed to concentrate my whole attention upon what I was reading, suddenly there would sound in the corridor the footsteps of a woman and the rustle of her dress. Instantly everything would escape my mind, and I would find it impossible to remain still any longer, however much I knew that the woman could only be either Gasha or my grandmother's old sewing-maid moving about in the corridor. "Yet suppose it should be SHE all at once?" I would say to myself. "Suppose IT is beginning now, and I were to lose it?" and, darting out into the corridor, I would find, each time, that it was only Gasha. Yet for long enough afterwards I could not recall my attention to my studies. A little spring had been touched in my head, and a strange mental ferment started afresh. Again, that evening I was sitting alone beside a tallow candle in my room. Suddenly I looked up for a moment—to snuff the candle, or to straighten myself in my chair—and at once became aware of nothing but the darkness in the corners and the blank of the open doorway. Then, I also became conscious how still the house was, and felt as though I could do nothing else than go on listening to that stillness, and gazing into the black square of that open doorway, and gradually sinking into a brown study as I sat there without moving. At intervals, however, I would get up, and go downstairs, and begin wandering through the empty rooms. Once I sat a long while in the small drawing-room as I listened to Gasha playing "The Nightingale" (with two fingers) on the piano in the large drawing-room, where a solitary candle burned. Later, when the moon was bright, I felt obliged to get out of bed and to lean out of the window, so that I might gaze into the garden, and at the lighted roof of the Shaposnikoff mansion, the straight tower of our parish church, and the dark shadows of the fence and the lilac-bush where they lay black upon the path. So long did I remain there that, when I at length returned to bed, it was ten o'clock in the morning before I could open my eyes again.

In short, had it not been for the tutors who came to give me lessons, as well as for St. Jerome (who at intervals, and very grudgingly, applied a spur to my self-conceit) and, most of all, for the desire to figure as "clever" in the eyes of my friend Nechludoff (who looked upon distinctions in University examinations as a matter of first-rate importance)—had it not been for all these things, I say, the spring and my new freedom would have combined to make me forget everything I had ever learnt, and so to go through the examinations to no purpose whatsoever.

X

The Examination in History

On the 16th of April I entered, for the first time, and under the wing of St. Jerome, the great hall of the University. I had driven there with St. Jerome in our smart phaeton and wearing the first frockcoat of my life, while the whole of my other clothes—even down to my socks and linen—were new and of a grander sort. When a Swiss waiter relieved me of my greatcoat, and I stood before him in all the beauty of my attire, I felt almost sorry to dazzle him so. Yet I had no sooner entered the bright, carpeted, crowded hall, and caught sight of hundreds of other young men in gymnasium (The Russian gymnasium = the English grammar or secondary school.) uniforms or frockcoats (of whom but a few threw me an indifferent glance), as well as, at the far end, of some solemn-looking professors who were seated on chairs or walking carelessly about among some tables, than I at once became disabused of the notion that I should attract the general attention, while the expression of my face, which at home, and even in the vestibule of the University buildings, had denoted only a kind of vague regret that I should have to present so important and distinguished an appearance, became exchanged for an expression of the most acute nervousness and dejection. However, I soon picked up again when I perceived sitting at one of the desks a very badly, untidily dressed gentleman who, though not really old, was almost entirely grey. He was occupying a seat quite at the back of the hall and a little apart from the rest, so I hastened to sit down beside him, and then fell to looking at the candidates for examination, and to forming conclusions about them. Many different figures and faces were there to be seen there; yet, in my opinion, they all seemed to divide themselves into three classes. First of all, there were youths like myself, attending for examination in the company of their parents or tutors. Among such I could see the youngest Iwin (accompanied by Frost) and Ilinka Grap (accompanied by his old father). All youths of this class wore the early beginnings of beards, sported prominent linen, sat quietly in their places, and never opened the books and notebooks which they had brought with them, but gazed at the professors and examination tables with ill-concealed nervousness. The second class of candidates were young men in gymnasium uniforms. Several of them had attained to the dignity of shaving, and most of them knew one another. They talked loudly, called the professors by their names and surnames, occupied themselves in getting their subjects ready, exchanged notebooks, climbed over desks, fetched themselves pies and sandwiches from the vestibule, and ate them then and there merely lowering their heads to the level of a desk for propriety's sake. Lastly, the third class of candidates (which seemed a small one) consisted of oldish men—some of them in frock coats, but the majority in jackets, and with no linen to be seen. These preserved a serious demeanour, sat by themselves, and had a very dingy look. The man who had afforded me consolation by being worse dressed than myself belonged to this class. Leaning forward upon his elbows, and running his fingers through his grey, dishevelled hair as he read some book or another, he had thrown me only a momentary glance—and that not a very friendly one—from a pair of glittering eyes. Then, as I sat down, he had frowned grimly, and stuck a shiny elbow out to prevent me from coming any nearer. On the other hand, the gymnasium men were over-sociable, and I felt rather afraid of their proximity. One of them did not hesitate to thrust a book into my hands, saying, "Give that to that fellow over there, will you?" while another of them exclaimed as he pushed past me, "By your leave, young fellow!" and a third made use of my shoulder as a prop when he wanted to scramble over a desk. All this seemed to me a little rough and unpleasant, for I looked upon myself as immensely superior to such fellows, and considered that they ought not to treat me with such familiarity. At length, the names began to be called out. The gymnasium men walked out boldly, answered their questions (apparently) well, and came back looking cheerful. My own class of candidates were much more diffident, as well as appeared to answer worse. Of the oldish men, some answered well, and some very poorly. When the name "Semenoff" was called out my neighbour with the grey hair and glittering eyes jostled me roughly, stepped over my legs, and went up to one of the examiners' tables. It was plain from the aspect of the professors that he answered well and with assurance, yet, on returning to his place, he did not wait to see where he was placed on the list, but quietly collected his notebooks and departed. Several times I shuddered at the sound of the voice calling out the names, but my turn did not come in exact alphabetical order, though already names had begun to be called beginning with "I."

"Ikonin and Tenieff!" suddenly shouted some one from the professors' end of the hall.

"Go on, Ikonin! You are being called," said a tall, red-faced gymnasium student near me. "But who is this BARtenieff or MORtenieff or somebody? I don't know him."

"It must be you," whispered St. Jerome loudly in my ear.

"My name is IRtenieff," I said to the red-faced student. "Do you think that was the name they were calling out?"

"Yes. Why on earth don't you go up?" he replied. "Lord, what a dandy!" he added under his breath, yet not so quietly but that I failed to hear the words as they came wafted to me from below the desk. In front of me walked Ikonin—a tall young man of about twenty-five, who was one of those whom I had classed as oldish men. He wore a tight brown frockcoat and a blue satin tie, and had wisps of flaxen hair carefully brushed over his collar in the peasant style. His appearance had already caught my attention when we were sitting among the desks, and had given me an impression that he was not bad-looking. Also I had noticed that he was very talkative. Yet what struck me most about his physiognomy was a tuft, of queer red hairs which he had under his chin, as well as, still more, a strange habit of continually unbuttoning his waistcoat and scratching his chest under his shirt.

Behind the table to which we were summoned sat three Professors, none of whom acknowledged our salutations. A youngish professor was shuffling a bundle of tickets like a pack of cards; another one, with a star on his frockcoat, was gazing hard at a gymnasium student, who was repeating something at great speed about Charles the Great, and adding to each of his sentences the word nakonetz (= the English colloquialism "you know.") while a third one—an old man in spectacles—proceeded to bend his head down as we approached, and, peering at us through his glasses, pointed silently to the tickets. I felt his glance go over both myself and Ikonin, and also felt sure that something about us had displeased him (perhaps it was Ikonin's red hairs), for, after taking another look at the pair of us, he motioned impatiently to us to be quick in taking our tickets. I felt vexed and offended—firstly, because none of the professors had responded to our bows, and, secondly, because they evidently coupled me with Ikonin under the one denomination of "candidates," and so were condemning me in advance on account of Ikonin's red hairs. I took my ticket boldly and made ready to answer, but the professor's eye passed over my head and alighted upon Ikonin.

Accordingly, I occupied myself in reading my ticket. The questions printed on it were all familiar to me, so, as I silently awaited my turn, I gazed at what was passing near me, Ikonin seemed in no way diffident—rather the reverse, for, in reaching for his ticket, he threw his body half-way across the table. Then he gave his long hair a shake, and rapidly conned over what was written on his ticket. I think he had just opened his mouth to answer when the professor with the star dismissed the gymnasium student with a word of commendation, and then turned and looked at Ikonin. At once the latter seemed taken back, and stopped short. For about two minutes there was a dead silence.

"Well?" said the professor in the spectacles.

Once more Ikonin opened his mouth, and once more remained silent.

"Come! You are not the only one to be examined. Do you mean to answer or do you not?" said the youngish professor, but Ikonin did not even look at him. He was gazing fixedly at his ticket and uttered not a single word. The professor in the spectacles scanned him through his glasses, then over them, then without them (for, indeed, he had time to take them off, to wipe their lenses carefully, and to replace them). Still not a word from Ikonin. All at once, however, a smile spread itself over his face, and he gave his long hair another shake. Next he reached across the table, laid down his ticket, looked at each of the professors in turn and then at myself, and finally, wheeling round on his heels, made a gesture with his hand and returned to the desks. The professors stared blankly at one another.

"Bless the fellow!" said the youngish professor. "What an original!"

It was now my turn to move towards the table, but the professors went on talking in undertones among themselves, as though they were unaware of my presence. At the moment, I felt firmly persuaded that the three of them were engrossed solely with the question of whether I should merely PASS the examination or whether I should pass it WELL, and that it was only swagger which made them pretend that they did not care either way, and behave as though they had not seen me.

When at length the professor in the spectacles turned to me with an air of indifference, and invited me to answer, I felt hurt, as I looked at him, to think that he should have so undeceived me: wherefore I answered brokenly at first. In time, however, things came easier to my tongue, and, inasmuch as all the questions bore upon Russian history (which I knew thoroughly), I ended with eclat, and even went so far, in my desire to convince the professors that I was not Ikonin and that they must not in anyway confound me with him, as to offer to draw a second ticket. The professor in the spectacles, however, merely nodded his head, said "That will do," and marked something in his register. On returning to the desks, I at once learnt from the gymnasium men (who somehow seemed to know everything) that I had been placed fifth.

My Examination in Mathematics

At the subsequent examinations, I made several new acquaintances in addition to the Graps (whom I considered unworthy of my notice) and Iwin (who for some reason or other avoided me). With some of these new friends I grew quite intimate, and even Ikonin plucked up sufficient courage to inform me, when we next met, that he would have to undergo re-examination in history—the reason for his failure this time being that the professor of that faculty had never forgiven him for last year's examination, and had, indeed, "almost killed" him for it. Semenoff (who was destined for the same faculty as myself—the faculty of mathematics) avoided every one up to the very close of the examinations. Always leaning forward upon his elbows and running his fingers through his grey hair, he sat silent and alone. Nevertheless, when called up for examination in mathematics (he had no companion to accompany him), he came out second. The first place was taken by a student from the first gymnasium—a tall, dark, lanky, pale-faced fellow who wore a black folded cravat and had his cheeks and forehead dotted all over with pimples. His hands were shapely and slender, but their nails were so bitten to the quick that the finger-ends looked as though they had been tied round with strips of thread. All this seemed to me splendid, and wholly becoming to a student of the first gymnasium. He spoke to every one, and we all made friends with him. To me in particular his walk, his every movement, his lips, his dark eyes, all seemed to have in them something extraordinary and magnetic.

On the day of the mathematical examination I arrived earlier than usual at the hall. I knew the syllabus well, yet there were two questions in the algebra which my tutor had managed to pass over, and which were therefore quite unknown to me. If I remember rightly, they were the Theory of Combinations and Newton's Binomial. I seated myself on one of the back benches and pored over the two questions, but, inasmuch as I was not accustomed to working in a noisy room, and had even less time for preparation than I had anticipated, I soon found it difficult to take in all that I was reading.

"Here he is. This way, Nechludoff," said Woloda's familiar voice behind me.

I turned and saw my brother and Dimitri—their gowns unbuttoned, and their hands waving a greeting to me—threading their way through the desks. A moment's glance would have sufficed to show any one that they were second-course students—persons to whom the University was as a second home. The mere look of their open gowns expressed at once disdain for the "mere candidate" and a knowledge that the "mere candidate's" soul was filled with envy and admiration of them. I was charmed to think that every one near me could now see that I knew two real second-course students: wherefore I hastened to meet them half-way.

Woloda, of course, could not help vaunting his superiority a little.

"Hullo, you smug!" he said. "Haven't you been examined yet?"

"No."

"Well, what are you reading? Aren't you sufficiently primed?"

"Yes, except in two questions. I don't understand them at all."

"Eh, what?"—and Woloda straightway began to expound to me Newton's Binomial, but so rapidly and unintelligibly that, suddenly reading in my eyes certain misgivings as to the soundness of his knowledge, he glanced also at Dimitri's face. Clearly, he saw the same misgivings there, for he blushed hotly, though still continuing his involved explanations.

"No; hold on, Woloda, and let me try and do it," put in Dimitri at length, with a glance at the professors' corner as he seated himself beside me.

I could see that my friend was in the best of humours. This was always the case with him when he was satisfied with himself, and was one of the things in him which I liked best. Inasmuch as he knew mathematics well and could speak clearly, he hammered the question so thoroughly into my head that I can remember it to this day. Hardly had he finished when St. Jerome said to me in a loud whisper, "A vous, Nicolas," and I followed Ikonin out from among the desks without having had an opportunity of going through the OTHER question of which I was ignorant. At the table which we now approached were seated two professors, while before the blackboard stood a gymnasium student, who was working some formula aloud, and knocking bits off the end of the chalk with his too vigorous strokes. He even continued writing after one of the Professors had said to him "Enough!" and bidden us draw our tickets. "Suppose I get the Theory of Combinations?" I thought to myself as my tremulous fingers took a ticket from among a bundle wrapped in torn paper. Ikonin, for his part, reached across the table with the same assurance, and the same sidelong movement of his whole body, as he had done at the previous examination. Taking the topmost ticket without troubling to make further selection, he just glanced at it, and then frowned angrily.

"I always draw this kind of thing," he muttered.

I looked at mine. Horrors! It was the Theory of Combinations!

"What have you got?" whispered Ikonin at this point.

I showed him.

"Oh, I know that," he said.

"Will you make an exchange, then?"

"No. Besides, it would be all the same for me if I did," he contrived to whisper just as the professor called us up to the blackboard. "I don't feel up to anything today."

"Then everything is lost!" I thought to myself. Instead of the brilliant result which I had anticipated I should be for ever covered with shame— more so even than Ikonin! Suddenly, under the very eyes of the professor, Ikonin turned to me, snatched my ticket out of my hands, and handed me his own. I looked at his ticket. It was Newton's Binomial!

The professor was a youngish man, with a pleasant, clever expression of face—an effect chiefly due to the prominence of the lower part of his forehead.

"What? Are you exchanging tickets, gentlemen?" he said.

"No. He only gave me his to look at, professor," answered Ikonin— and, sure enough, the word "professor" was the last word that he uttered there. Once again, he stepped backwards towards me from the table, once again he looked at each of the professors in turn and then at myself, once again he smiled faintly, and once again he shrugged his shoulders as much as to say, "It is no use, my good sirs." Then he returned to the desks. Subsequently, I learnt that this was the third year he had vainly attempted to matriculate.

I answered my question well, for I had just read it up; and the professor, kindly informing me that I had done even better than was required, placed me fifth.

XII

My Examination in Latin

All went well until my examination in Latin. So far, a gymnasium student stood first on the list, Semenoff second, and myself third. On the strength of it I had begun to swagger a little, and to think that, for all my youth, I was not to be despised.

From the first day of the examinations, I had heard every one speak with awe of the Professor of Latin, who appeared to be some sort of a wild beast who battened on the financial ruin of young men (of those, that is to say, who paid their own fees) and spoke only in the Greek and Latin tongues. However, St. Jerome, who had coached me in Latin, spoke encouragingly, and I myself thought that, since I could translate Cicero and certain parts of Horace without the aid of a lexicon, I should do no worse than the rest. Yet things proved otherwise. All the morning the air had been full of rumours concerning the tribulations of candidates who had gone up before me: rumours of how one young fellow had been accorded a nought, another one a single mark only, a third one greeted with abuse and threatened with expulsion, and so forth. Only Semenoff and the first gymnasium student had, as usual, gone up quietly, and returned to their seats with five marks credited to their names. Already I felt a prescience of disaster when Ikonin and myself found ourselves summoned to the little table at which the terrible professor sat in solitary grandeur.

The terrible professor turned out to be a little thin, bilious-looking man with hair long and greasy and a face expressive of extraordinary sullenness. Handing Ikonin a copy of Cicero's Orations, he bid him translate. To my great astonishment Ikonin not only read off some of the Latin, but even managed to construe a few lines to the professor's prompting. At the same time, conscious of my superiority over such a feeble companion, I could not help smiling a little, and even looking rather contemptuous, when it came to a question of analysis, and Ikonin, as on previous occasions, plunged into a silence which promised never to end. I had hoped to please the professor by that knowing, slightly sarcastic smile of mine, but, as a matter of fact, I contrived to do quite the contrary.

"Evidently you know better than he, since you are laughing," he said to me in bad Russian. "Well, we shall see. Tell me the answer, then."

Later I learnt that the professor was Ikonin's guardian, and that Ikonin actually lived with him. I lost no time in answering the question in syntax which had been put to Ikonin, but the professor only pulled a long face and turned away from me.

"Well, your turn will come presently, and then we shall see how much you know," he remarked, without looking at me, but proceeding to explain to Ikonin the point on which he had questioned him.

"That will do," he added, and I saw him put down four marks to Ikonin in his register. "Come!" I thought to myself. "He cannot be so strict after all."

When Ikonin had taken his departure the professor spent fully five minutes—five minutes which seemed to me five hours—in setting his books and tickets in order, in blowing his nose, in adjusting and sprawling about on his chair, in gazing down the hall, and in looking here, there, and everywhere—in doing everything, in fact, except once letting his eye rest upon me. Yet even that amount of dissimulation did not seem to satisfy him, for he next opened a book, and pretended to read it, for all the world as though I were not there at all. I moved a little nearer him, and gave a cough.

"Ah, yes! You too, of course! Well, translate me something," he remarked, handing me a book of some kind. "But no; you had better take this," and, turning over the leaves of a Horace, he indicated to me a passage which I should never have imagined possible of translation.

"I have not prepared this," I said.

"Oh! Then you only wish to answer things which you have got by heart, do you? Indeed? No, no; translate me that."

I started to grope for the meaning of the passage, but each questioning look which I threw at the professor was met by a shake of the head, a profound sigh, and an exclamation of "No, no!" Finally he banged the book to with such a snap that he caught his finger between the covers. Angrily releasing it, he handed me a ticket containing questions in grammar, and, flinging himself back in his chair, maintained a menacing silence. I should have tried to answer the questions had not the expression of his face so clogged my tongue that nothing seemed to come from it right.

"No, no! That's not it at all!" he suddenly exclaimed in his horrible accent as he altered his posture to one of leaning forward upon the table and playing with the gold signet-ring which was nearly slipping from the little finger of his left hand. "That is not the way to prepare for serious study, my good sir. Fellows like yourself think that, once they have a gown and a blue collar to their backs, they have reached the summit of all things and become students. No, no, my dear sir. A subject needs to be studied FUNDAMENTALLY," and so on, and so on.

During this speech (which was uttered with a clipped sort of intonation) I went on staring dully at his lowered eyelids. Beginning with a fear lest I should lose my place as third on the list, I went on to fear lest I should pass at all. Next, these feelings became reinforced by a sense of injustice, injured self-respect, and unmerited humiliation, while the contempt which I felt for the professor as some one not quite (according to my ideas) "comme il faut"—a fact which I deduced from the shortness, strength, and roundness of his nails—flared up in me more and more and turned all my other feelings to sheer animosity. Happening, presently, to glance at me, and to note my quivering lips and tear-filled eyes, he seemed to interpret my agitation as a desire to be accorded my marks and dismissed: wherefore, with an air of relenting, he said (in the presence of another professor who had just approached):

"Very well; I will accord you a 'pass'" (which signified two marks), "although you do not deserve it. I do so simply out of consideration for your youth, and in the hope that, when you begin your University career, you will learn to be less light-minded."

The concluding phrase, uttered in the hearing of the other professor (who at once turned his eyes upon me, as though remarking, "There! You see, young man!") completed my discomfiture. For a moment, a mist swam before my eyes—a mist in which the terrible professor seemed to be far away, as he sat at his table while for an instant a wild idea danced through my brain. "What if I DID do such a thing?" I thought to myself. "What would come of it?" However, I did not do the thing in question, but, on the contrary, made a bow of peculiar reverence to each of the professors, and with a slight smile on my face—presumably the same smile as that with which I had derided Ikonin—turned away from the table.

This piece of unfairness affected me so powerfully at the time that, had I been a free agent, I should have attended for no more examinations. My ambition was gone (since now I could not possibly be third), and I therefore let the other examinations pass without any exertion, or even agitation, on my part. In the general list I still stood fourth, but that failed to interest me, since I had reasoned things out to myself, and come to the conclusion that to try for first place was stupid—even "bad form:" that, in fact, it was better to pass neither very well nor very badly, as Woloda had done. This attitude I decided to maintain throughout the whole of my University career, notwithstanding that it was the first point on which my opinion had differed from that of my friend Dimitri.

Yet, to tell the truth, my thoughts were already turning towards a uniform, a "mortar-board," and the possession of a drozhki of my own, a room of my own, and, above all, freedom of my own. And certainly the prospect had its charm.

XIII

I Become Grown-Up

When, on May 8th, I returned home from the final, the divinity, examination, I found my acquaintance, the foreman from Rozonoff's, awaiting me. He had called once before to fit me for my gown, as well as for a tunic of glossy black cloth (the lapels of which were, on that occasion, only sketched in chalk), but today he had come to bring me the clothes in their finished state, with their gilt buttons wrapped in tissue paper.

Donning the garments, and finding them splendid (notwithstanding that St. Jerome assured me that the back of the tunic wrinkled badly), I went downstairs with a complacent smile which I was powerless to banish from my face, and sought Woloda, trying the while to affect unconsciousness of the admiring looks of the servants, who came darting out of the hall and corridor to gaze upon me with ravished eyes. Gabriel, the butler, overtook me in the salle, and, after congratulating me with much empressement, handed me, according to instructions from my father, four bank-notes, as well as informed me that Papa had also given orders that, from that day forth, the groom Kuzma, the phaeton, and the bay horse Krassavchik were to be entirely at my disposal. I was so overjoyed at this not altogether expected good-fortune that I could no longer feign indifference in Gabriel's presence, but, flustered and panting, said the first thing which came into my head ("Krassavchik is a splendid trotter," I think it was). Then, catching sight of the various heads protruding from the doors of the hall and corridor, I felt that I could bear no more, and set off running at full speed across the salle, dressed as I was in the new tunic, with its shining gilt buttons. Just as I burst into Woloda's room, I heard behind me the voices of Dubkoff and Nechludoff, who had come to congratulate me, as well as to propose a dinner somewhere and the drinking of much champagne in honour of my matriculation. Dimitri informed me that, though he did not care for champagne, he would nevertheless join us that evening and drink my health, while Dubkoff remarked that I looked almost like a colonel, and Woloda omitted to congratulate me at all, merely saying in an acid way that he supposed we should now—i.e. in two days time—be off into the country. The truth was that Woloda, though pleased at my matriculation, did not altogether like my becoming as grown-up as himself. St. Jerome, who also joined us at this moment, said in a very pompous manner that his duties were now ended, and that, although he did not know whether they had been well done or ill, at least he had done his best, and must depart tomorrow to his Count's. In replying to their various remarks I could feel, in spite of myself, a pleased, agreeable, faintly self-sufficient smile playing over my countenance, as well as could remark that that smile, communicated itself to those to whom I was speaking.

So here was I without a tutor, yet with my own private drozhki, my name printed on the list of students, a sword and belt of my own, and a chance of an occasional salute from officials! In short, I was grownup and, I suppose, happy.

Finally, we arranged to go out and dine at five o'clock, but since Woloda presently went off to Dubkoff's, and Dimitri disappeared in his usual fashion (saying that there was something he Must do before dinner), I was left with two whole hours still at my disposal. For a time I walked through the rooms of the house, and looked at myself in all the mirrors—firstly with the tunic buttoned, then with it unbuttoned, and lastly with only the top button fastened. Each time it looked splendid. Eventually, though anxious not to show any excess of delight, I found myself unable to refrain from crossing over to the coach-house and stables to gaze at Krassovchik, Kuzma, and the drozhki. Then I returned and once more began my tour of the rooms, where I looked at myself in all the mirrors as before, and counted my money over in my pocket—my face smiling happily the while. Yet not an hour had elapsed before I began to feel slightly ennuye—to feel a shade of regret that no one was present to see me in my splendid position. I began to long for life and movement, and so sent out orders for the drozhki to be got ready, since I had made up my mind to drive to the Kuznetski Bridge and make some purchases.

In this connection I recalled how, after matriculating, Woloda had gone and bought himself a lithograph of horses by Victor Adam and some pipes and tobacco: wherefore I felt that I too must do the same. Amid glances showered upon me from every side, and with the sunlight reflected from my buttons, cap-badge, and sword, I drove to the Kuznetski Bridge, where, halting at a Picture shop, I entered it with my eyes looking to every side. It was not precisely horses by Adam which I meant to buy, since I did not wish to be accused of too closely imitating Woloda; wherefore, out of shame for causing the obsequious shopmen such agitation as I appeared to do, I made a hasty selection, and pitched upon a water-colour of a woman's head which I saw displayed in the window—price twenty roubles. Yet no sooner had I paid the twenty roubles over the counter than my heart smote me for having put two such beautifully dressed shop-assistants to so much trouble for such a trifle. Moreover, I fancied that they were regarding me with some disdain. Accordingly, in my desire to show them what manner of man I was, I turned my attention to a silver trifle which I saw displayed in a show-case, and, recognising that it was a porte-crayon (price eighteen roubles), requested that it should forthwith be wrapped in paper for me. Next, the money paid, and the information acquired that splendid pipes and tobacco were to be obtained in an adjacent emporium, I bowed to the two shopmen politely, and issued into the street with the picture under my arm. At the shop next door (which had painted on its sign-board a negro smoking a cigar) I bought (likewise out of a desire to imitate no one) some Turkish tobacco, a Stamboul hookah, and two pipes. On coming out of the shop, I had just entered the drozhki when I caught sight of Semenoff, who was walking hurriedly along the pavement with his head bent down. Vexed that he should not have recognised me, I called out to him pretty loudly, "Hold on a minute!" and, whipping up the drozhki, soon overtook him.

"How do you do?" I said.

"My respects to you," he replied, but without stopping.

"Why are you not in your University uniform?" I next inquired.

At this he stopped short with a frown, and parted his white teeth as though the sun were hurting his eyes. The next moment, however, he threw a glance of studied indifference at my drozhki and uniform, and continued on his way.

From the Kuznetski Bridge, I drove to a confectioner's in Tverskaia Street, and, much as I should have liked it to be supposed that it was the newspapers which most interested me, I had no choice but to begin falling upon tartlet after tartlet. In fact, for all my bashfulness before a gentleman who kept regarding me with some curiosity from behind a newspaper, I ate with great swiftness a tartlet of each of the eight different sorts which the confectioner kept.

On reaching home, I experienced a slight touch of stomach-ache, but paid no attention to it, and set to work to inspect my purchases.

Of these, the picture so much displeased me that, instead of having it framed and hung in my room, as Woloda had done with his, I took pains to hide it behind a chest of drawers, where no one could see it. Likewise, though I also found the porte-crayon distasteful, I was able, as I laid it on my table, to comfort myself with the thought that it was at least a SILVER article—so much capital, as it were—and likely to be very useful to a student. As for the smoking things, I decided to put them into use at once, and try their capabilities.

Unsealing the four packages, and carefully filling the Stamboul pipe with some fine-cut, reddish-yellow Turkish tobacco, I applied a hot cinder to it, and, taking the mouthpiece between my first and second fingers (a position of the hand which greatly caught my fancy), started to inhale the smoke.

The smell of the tobacco seemed delightful, yet something burnt my mouth and caught me by the breath. Nevertheless, I hardened my heart, and continued to draw abundant fumes into my interior. Then I tried blowing rings and retaining the smoke. Soon the room became filled with blue vapours, while the pipe started to crackle and the tobacco to fly out in sparks. Presently, also, I began to feel a smarting in my mouth and a giddiness in my head. Accordingly, I was on the point of stopping and going to look at myself and my pipe in the mirror, when, to my surprise, I found myself staggering about. The room was whirling round and round, and as I peered into the mirror (which I reached only with some difficulty) I perceived that my face was as white as a sheet. Hardly had I thrown myself down upon a sofa when such nausea and faintness swept over me that, making up my mind that the pipe had proved my death, I expected every moment to expire. Terribly frightened, I tried to call out for some one to come and help me, and to send for the doctor.

However, this panic of mine did not last long, for I soon understood what the matter with me was, and remained lying on the sofa with a racking headache and my limbs relaxed as I stared dully at the stamp on the package of tobacco, the Pipe-tube coiled on the floor, and the odds and ends of tobacco and confectioner's tartlets which were littered about. "Truly," I thought to myself in my dejection and disillusionment, "I cannot be quite grown-up if I cannot smoke as other fellows do, and should be fated never to hold a chibouk between my first and second fingers, or to inhale and puff smoke through a flaxen moustache!"

When Dimitri called for me at five o'clock, he found me in this unpleasant predicament. After drinking a glass of water, however, I felt nearly recovered, and ready to go with him.

"So much for your trying to smoke!" said he as he gazed at the remnants of my debauch. "It is a silly thing to do, and waste of money as well. I long ago promised myself never to smoke. But come along; we have to call for Dubkoff."

XIV

How Woloda and Dubkoff Amused Themselves

The moment that Dimitri entered my room I perceived from his face, manner of walking, and the signs which, in him, denoted ill-humour—a blinking of the eyes and a grim holding of his head to one side, as though to straighten his collar—that he was in the coldly-correct frame of mind which was his when he felt dissatisfied with himself. It was a frame of mind, too, which always produced a chilling effect upon my feelings towards him. Of late I had begun to observe and appraise my friend's character a little more, but our friendship had in no way suffered from that, since it was still too young and strong for me to be able to look upon Dimitri as anything but perfect, no matter in what light I regarded him. In him there were two personalities, both of which I thought beautiful. One, which I loved devotedly, was kind, mild, forgiving, gay, and conscious of being those various things. When he was in this frame of mind his whole exterior, the very tone of his voice, his every movement, appeared to say: "I am kind and good-natured, and rejoice in being so, and every one can see that I so rejoice." The other of his two personalities—one which I had only just begun to apprehend, and before the majesty of which I bowed in spirit—was that of a man who was cold, stern to himself and to others, proud, religious to the point of fanaticism, and pedantically moral. At the present moment he was, as I say, this second personality.

With that frankness which constituted a necessary condition of our relations I told him, as soon as we entered the drozhki, how much it depressed and hurt me to see him, on this my fete-day in a frame of mind so irksome and disagreeable to me.

"What has upset you so?" I asked him. "Will you not tell me?"

"My dear Nicolas," was his slow reply as he gave his head a nervous twitch to one side and blinked his eyes, "since I have given you my word never to conceal anything from you, you have no reason to suspect me of secretiveness. One cannot always be in exactly the same mood, and if I seem at all put out, that is all there is to say about it."

"What a marvellously open, honourable character his is!" I thought to myself, and dropped the subject.

We drove the rest of the way to Dubkoff's in silence. Dubkoff's flat was an unusually fine one—or, at all events, so it seemed to me. Everywhere were rugs, pictures, gardenias, striped hangings, photographs, and curved settees, while on the walls hung guns, pistols, pouches, and the mounted heads of wild beasts. It was the appearance of this apartment which made me aware whom, it was that Woloda had imitated in the scheme of his own sitting-room. We found Dubkoff and Woloda engaged in cards, while seated also at the table, and watching the game with close attention, was a gentleman whom I did not know, but who appeared to be of no great importance, judging by the modesty of his attitude. Dubkoff himself was in a silk dressing-gown and soft slippers, while Woloda—seated opposite him on a divan—was in his shirtsleeves, as well as (to judge by his flushed face and the impatient, cursory glance which he gave us for a second as he looked up from the cards) much taken up with the game. On seeing me, he reddened still more.

"Well, it is for you to deal," he remarked to Dubkoff. In an instant I divined that he did not altogether relish my becoming acquainted with the fact that he gambled. Yet his expression had nothing in it of confusion—only a look which seemed to me to say: "Yes, I play cards, and if you are surprised at that, it is only because you are so young. There is nothing wrong about it—it is a necessity at our age." Yes, I at once divined and understood that.

Instead of dealing, however, Dubkoff rose and shook hands with us; after which he bade us both be seated, and then offered us pipes, which we declined.

"Here is our Diplomat, then—the hero of the day!" he said to me, "Good Lord! how you look like a colonel!"

"H-m!" I muttered in reply, though once more feeling a complacent smile overspread my countenance.

I stood in that awe of Dubkoff which a sixteen-year-old boy naturally feels for a twenty-seven-year-old man of whom his elders say that he is a very clever young man who can dance well and speak French, and who, though secretly despising one's youth, endeavours to conceal the fact. Yet, despite my respect for him, I somehow found it difficult and uncomfortable, throughout my acquaintanceship with him, to look him in the eyes, I have since remarked that there are three kinds of men whom I cannot face easily, namely those who are much better than myself, those who are much worse, and those between whom and myself there is a mutual determination not to mention some particular thing of which we are both aware. Dubkoff may have been a much better fellow than myself, or he may have been a much worse; but the point was that he lied very frequently without recognising the fact that I was aware of his doing so, yet had determined not to mention it.

"Let us play another round," said Woloda, hunching one shoulder after the manner of Papa, and reshuffling the cards.

"How persistent you are!" said Dubkoff. "We can play all we want to afterwards. Well, one more round, then."

During the play, I looked at their hands. Woloda's hands were large and red, whilst in the crook of the thumb and the way in which the other fingers curved themselves round the cards as he held them they so exactly resembled Papa's that now and then I could not help thinking that Woloda purposely held the cards thus so as to look the more like a grownup. Yet the next moment, looking at his face, I could see that he had not a thought in his mind beyond the game. Dubkoff's hands, on the contrary, were small, puffy, and inclined to clench themselves, as well as extremely neat and small-fingered. They were just the kind of hands which generally display rings, and which are most to be seen on persons who are both inclined to use them and fond of objets de vertu.

Woloda must have lost, for the gentleman who was watching the play remarked that Vladimir Petrovitch had terribly bad luck, while Dubkoff reached for a note book, wrote something in it, and then, showing Woloda what he had written, said:

"Is that right?"

"Yes." said Woloda, glancing with feigned carelessness at the note book. "Now let us go."

Woloda took Dubkoff, and I gave Dimitri a lift in my drozhki.

"What were they playing at?" I inquired of Dimitri.

"At piquet. It is a stupid game. In fact, all such games are stupid."

"And were they playing for much?"

"No, not very much, but more than they ought to."

"Do you ever play yourself?"

"No; I swore never to do so; but Dubkoff will play with any one he can get hold of."

"He ought not to do that," I remarked. "So Woloda does not play so well as he does?"

"Perhaps Dubkoff ought not to, as you say, yet there is nothing especially bad about it all. He likes playing, and plays well, but he is a good fellow all the same."

"I had no idea of this," I said.

"We must not think ill of him," concluded Dimitri, "since he is a simply splendid fellow. I like him very much, and always shall like him, in spite of his weakness."

For some reason or another the idea occurred to me that, just BECAUSE Dimitri stuck up so stoutly for Dubkoff, he neither liked nor respected him in reality, but was determined, out of stubbornness and a desire not to be accused of inconstancy, never to own to the fact. He was one of those people who love their friends their life long, not so much because those friends remain always dear to them, as because, having once—possibly mistakenly—liked a person, they look upon it as dishonourable to cease ever to do so.

XV

I Am Feted at Dinner

Dubkoff and Woloda knew every one at the restaurant by name, and every one, from the waiters to the proprietor, paid them great respect. No time was lost in allotting us a private room, where a bottle of iced champagne-upon which I tried to look with as much indifference as I could—stood ready waiting for us, and where we were served with a most wonderful repast selected by Dubkoff from the French menu. The meal went off most gaily and agreeably, notwithstanding that Dubkoff, as usual, told us blood-curdling tales of doubtful veracity (among others, a tale of how his grandmother once shot dead three robbers who were attacking her—a recital at which I blushed, closed my eyes, and turned away from the narrator), and that Woloda reddened visibly whenever I opened my mouth to speak—which was the more uncalled for on his part, seeing that never once, so far as I can remember, did I say anything shameful. After we had been given champagne, every one congratulated me, and I drank "hands across" with Dimitri and Dubkoff, and wished them joy. Since, however, I did not know to whom the bottle of champagne belonged (it was explained to me later that it was common property), I considered that, in return, I ought to treat my friends out of the money which I had never ceased to finger in my pocket. Accordingly, I stealthily extracted a ten-rouble note, and, beckoning the waiter to my side, handed him the money, and told him in a whisper (yet not so softly but that every one could hear me, seeing that every one was staring at me in dead silence) to "bring, if you please, a half-bottle of champagne." At this Woloda reddened again, and began to fidget so violently, and to gaze upon myself and every one else with such a distracted air, that I felt sure I had somehow put my foot in it. However, the half-bottle came, and we drank it with great gusto. After that, things went on merrily. Dubkoff continued his unending fairy tales, while Woloda also told funny stories—and told them well, too—in a way I should never have credited him: so that our laughter rang long and loud. Their best efforts lay in imitation, and in variants of a certain well-known saw. "Have you ever been abroad?" one would say to the other, for instance. "No," the one interrogated would reply, "but my brother plays the fiddle." Such perfection had the pair attained in this species of comic absurdity that they could answer any question by its means, while they would also endeavour to unite two absolutely unconnected matters without a previous question having been asked at all, yet say everything with a perfectly serious face and produce a most comic effect. I too began to try to be funny, but as soon as ever I spoke they either looked at me askance or did not look at me until I had finished: so that my anecdotes fell flat. Yet, though Dubkoff always remarked, "Our DIPLOMAT is lying, brother," I felt so exhilarated with the champagne and the company of my elders that the remark scarcely touched me. Only Dimitri, though he drank level with the rest of us, continued in the same severe, serious frame of mind—a fact which put a certain check upon the general hilarity.

"Now, look here, gentlemen," said Dubkoff at last. "After dinner we ought to take the DIPLOMAT in hand. How would it be for him to go with us to see Auntie? There we could put him through his paces."

"Ah, but Nechludoff will not go there," objected Woloda.

"O unbearable, insupportable man of quiet habits that you are!" cried Dubkoff, turning to Dimitri. "Yet come with us, and you shall see what an excellent lady my dear Auntie is."

"I will neither go myself nor let him go," replied Dimitri.

"Let whom go? The DIPLOMAT? Why, you yourself saw how he brightened up at the very mention of Auntie."

"It is not so much that I WILL NOT LET HIM go," continued Dimitri, rising and beginning to pace the room without looking at me, "as that I neither wish him nor advise him to go. He is not a child now, and if he must go he can go alone—without you. Surely you are ashamed of this, Dubkoff?—ashamed of always wanting others to do all the wrong things that you yourself do?"

"But what is there so very wrong in my inviting you all to come and take a cup of tea with my Aunt?" said Dubkoff, with a wink at Woloda. "If you don't like us going, it is your affair; yet we are going all the same. Are you coming, Woloda?"

"Yes, yes," assented Woloda. "We can go there, and then return to my rooms and continue our piquet."

"Do you want to go with them or not?" said Dimitri, approaching me.

"No," I replied, at the same time making room for him to sit down beside me on the divan. "I did not wish to go in any case, and since you advise me not to, nothing on earth will make me go now. Yet," I added a moment later, "I cannot honestly say that I have No desire to go. All I say is that I am glad I am not going."

"That is right," he said. "Live your own life, and do not dance to any one's piping. That is the better way."

This little tiff not only failed to mar our hilarity, but even increased it. Dimitri suddenly reverted to the kindly mood which I loved best—so great (as I afterwards remarked on more than one occasion) was the influence which the consciousness of having done a good deed exercised upon him. At the present moment the source of his satisfaction was the fact that he had stopped my expedition to "Auntie's." He grew extraordinarily gay, called for another bottle of champagne (which was against his rules), invited some one who was a perfect stranger into our room, plied him with wine, sang "Gaudeamus igitur," requested every one to join him in the chorus, and proposed that we should and rink at the Sokolniki. (Mews.)

"Let us enjoy ourselves tonight," he said with a laugh. "It is in honour of his matriculation that you now see me getting drunk for the first time in my life."

Yet somehow this merriment sat ill upon him. He was like some good-natured father or tutor who is pleased with his young charges, and lets himself go for their amusement, yet at the same time tries to show them that one can enjoy oneself decently and in an honourable manner. However, his unexpected gaiety had an infectious influence upon myself and my companions, and the more so because each of us had now drunk about half a bottle of champagne.

It was in this pleasing frame of mind that I went out into the main salon to smoke a cigarette which Dubkoff had given me. In rising I noticed that my head seemed to swim a little, and that my legs and arms retained their natural positions only when I bent my thoughts determinedly upon them. At other moments my legs would deviate from the straight line, and my arms describe strange gestures. I concentrated my whole attention upon the members in question, forced my hands first to raise themselves and button my tunic, and then to smooth my hair (though they ruffled my locks in doing so), and lastly commanded my legs to march me to the door—a function which they duly performed, though at one time with too much reluctance, and at another with too much ABANDON (the left leg, in particular, coming to a halt every moment on tiptoe). Some one called out to me, "Where are you going to? They will bring you a cigar-light directly," but I guessed the voice to be Woloda's, and, feeling satisfied, somehow, that I had succeeded in divining the fact, merely smiled airily in reply, and continued on my way.

XVI

The Quarrel

In the main salon I perceived sitting at a small table a short, squat gentleman of the professional type. He had a red moustache, and was engaged in eating something or another, while by his side sat a tall, clean-shaven individual with whom he was carrying on a conversation in French. Somehow the aspect of these two persons displeased me; yet I decided, for all that, to light my cigarette at the candelabrum which was standing before them. Looking from side to side, to avoid meeting their gaze, I approached the table, and applied my cigarette to the flame. When it was fairly alight, I involuntarily threw a glance at the gentleman who was eating, and found his grey eyes fixed upon me with an expression of intense displeasure. Just as I was turning away his red moustache moved a little, and he said in French:

"I do not like people to smoke when I am dining, my good sir."

I murmured something inaudible.

"No, I do not like it at all," he went on sternly, and with a glance at his clean-shaven companion, as though inviting him to admire the way in which he was about to deal with me. "I do not like it, my good sir, nor do I like people who have the impudence to puff their smoke up one's very nose."

By this time I had gathered that it was myself he was scolding, and at first felt as though I had been altogether in the wrong.

"I did not mean to inconvenience you," I said.

"Well, if you did not suppose you were being impertinent, at least I did! You are a cad, young sir!" he shouted in reply.

"But what right have you to shout at me like that?" I exclaimed, feeling that it was now He that was insulting Me, and growing angry accordingly.

"This much right," he replied, "that I never allow myself to be overlooked by any one, and that I always teach young fellows like yourself their manners. What is your name, young sir, and where do you live?"

At this I felt so hurt that my teeth chattered, and I felt as though I were choking. Yet all the while I was conscious of being in the wrong, and so, instead of offering any further rudeness to the offended one, humbly told him my name and address.

"And MY name, young sir," he returned, "is Kolpikoff, and I will trouble you to be more polite to me in future.—However, You will hear from me again" ("vous aurez de mes nouvelles"—the conversation had been carried on wholly in French), was his concluding remark.

To this I replied, "I shall be delighted," with an infusion of as much hauteur as I could muster into my tone. Then, turning on my heel, I returned with my cigarette—which had meanwhile gone out—to our own room.

I said nothing, either to my brother or my friends, about what had happened (and the more so because they were at that moment engaged in a dispute of their own), but sat down in a corner to think over the strange affair. The words, "You are a cad, young sir," vexed me more and more the longer that they sounded in my ears. My tipsiness was gone now, and, in considering my conduct during the dispute, the uncomfortable thought came over me that I had behaved like a coward.

"Yet what right had he to attack me?" I reflected. "Why did he not simply intimate to me that I was annoying him? After all, it may have been he that was in the wrong. Why, too, when he called me a young cad, did I not say to him, 'A cad, my good sir, is one who takes offence'? Or why did I not simply tell him to hold his tongue? That would have been the better course. Or why did I not challenge him to a duel? No, I did none of those things, but swallowed his insults like a wretched coward."

Still the words, "You are a cad, young sir," kept sounding in my ears with maddening iteration. "I cannot leave things as they are," I at length decided as I rose to my feet with the fixed intention of returning to the gentleman and saying something outrageous to him—perhaps, also, of breaking the candelabrum over his head if occasion offered. Yet, though I considered the advisability of this last measure with some pleasure, it was not without a good deal of trepidation that I re-entered the main salon. As luck would have it, M. Kolpikoff was no longer there, but only a waiter engaged in clearing the table. For a moment I felt like telling the waiter the whole story, and explaining to him my innocence in the matter, but for some reason or another I thought better of it, and once more returned, in the same hazy condition of mind, to our own room.

"What has become of our DIPLOMAT?" Dubkoff was just saying. "Upon him now hang the fortunes of Europe."

"Oh, leave me alone," I said, turning moodily away. Then, as I paced the room, something made me begin to think that Dubkoff was not altogether a good fellow. "There is nothing very much to admire in his eternal jokes and his nickname of 'DIPLOMAT,'" I reflected. "All he thinks about is to win money from Woloda and to go and see his 'Auntie.' There is nothing very nice in all that. Besides, everything he says has a touch of blackguardism in it, and he is forever trying to make people laugh. In my opinion he is simply stupid when he is not absolutely a brute." I spent about five minutes in these reflections, and felt my enmity towards Dubkoff continually increasing. For his part, he took no notice of me, and that angered me the more. I actually felt vexed with Woloda and Dimitri because they went on talking to him.

"I tell you what, gentlemen: the DIPLOMAT ought to be christened," said Dubkoff suddenly, with a glance and a smile which seemed to me derisive, and even treacherous. "Yet, O Lord, what a poor specimen he is!"

"You yourself ought to be christened, and you yourself are a sorry specimen!" I retorted with an evil smile, and actually forgetting to address him as "thou." (In Russian as in French, the second person singular is the form of speech used between intimate friends.)

This reply evidently surprised Dubkoff, but he turned away good-humouredly, and went on talking to Woloda and Dimitri. I tried to edge myself into the conversation, but, since I felt that I could not keep it up, I soon returned to my corner, and remained there until we left.

When the bill had been paid and wraps were being put on, Dubkoff turned to Dimitri and said: "Whither are Orestes and Pedalion going now? Home, I suppose, to talk about love. Well, let Us go and see my dear Auntie. That will be far more entertaining than your sour company."

"How dare you speak like that, and laugh at us?" I burst out as I approached him with clenched fists. "How dare you laugh at feelings which you do not understand? I will not have you do it! Hold your tongue!" At this point I had to hold my own, for I did not know what to say next, and was, moreover, out of breath with excitement. At first Dubkoff was taken aback, but presently he tried to laugh it off, and to take it as a joke. Finally I was surprised to see him look crestfallen, and lower his eyes.

"I NEVER laugh at you or your feelings. It is merely my way of speaking," he said evasively.

"Indeed?" I cried; yet the next moment I felt ashamed of myself and sorry for him, since his flushed, downcast face had in it no other expression than one of genuine pain.

"What is the matter with you?" said Woloda and Dimitri simultaneously. "No one was trying to insult you."

"Yes, he DID try to insult me!" I replied.

"What an extraordinary fellow your brother is!" said Dubkoff to Woloda. At that moment he was passing out of the door, and could not have heard what I said. Possibly I should have flung myself after him and offered him further insult, had it not been that just at that moment the waiter who had witnessed my encounter with Kolpikoff handed me my greatcoat, and I at once quietened down—merely making such a pretence of having had a difference with Dimitri as was necessary to make my sudden appeasement appear nothing extraordinary. Next day, when I met Dubkoff at Woloda's, the quarrel was not raked up, yet he and I still addressed each other as "you," and found it harder than ever to look one another in the face.

The remembrance of my scene with Kolpikoff—who, by the way, never sent me "de ses nouvelles," either the following day or any day afterwards—remained for years a keen and unpleasant memory. Even so much as five years after it had happened I would begin fidgeting and muttering to myself whenever I remembered the unavenged insult, and was fain to comfort myself with the satisfaction of recollecting the sort of young fellow I had shown myself to be in my subsequent affair with Dubkoff. In fact, it was only later still that I began to regard the matter in another light, and both to recall with comic appreciation my passage of arms with Kolpikoff, and to regret the undeserved affront which I had offered my good friend Dubkoff.

When, at a later hour on the evening of the dinner, I told Dimitri of my affair with Kolpikoff, whose exterior I described in detail, he was astounded.

"That is the very man!" he cried. "Don't you know that this precious Kolpikoff is a known scamp and sharper, as well as, above all things, a coward, and that he was expelled from his regiment by his brother officers because, having had his face slapped, he would not fight? But how came you to let him get away?" he added, with a kindly smile and glance. "Surely he could not have said more to you than he did when he called you a cad?"

"No," I admitted with a blush.

"Well, it was not right, but there is no great harm done," said Dimitri consolingly.

Long afterwards, when thinking the matter over at leisure, I suddenly came to the conclusion that it was quite possible that Kolpikoff took the opportunity of vicariously wiping off upon me the slap in the face which he had once received, just as I myself took the opportunity of vicariously wiping off upon the innocent Dubkoff the epithet "cad" which Kolpikoff had just applied to me.

XVII

I Get Ready to Pay Some Calls

On awaking next morning my first thoughts were of the affair with Kolpikoff. Once again I muttered to myself and stamped about the room, but there was no help for it. Today was the last day that I was to spend in Moscow, and it was to be spent, by Papa's orders, in my paying a round of calls which he had written out for me on a piece of paper—his first solicitude on our account being not so much for our morals or our education as for our due observance of the convenances. On the piece of paper was written in his swift, broken hand-writing: "(1) Prince Ivan Ivanovitch Without Fail; (2) the Iwins Without Fail; (3) Prince Michael; (4) the Princess Nechludoff and Madame Valakhina if you wish." Of course I was also to call upon my guardian, upon the rector, and upon the professors.

These last-mentioned calls, however, Dimitri advised me not to pay: saying that it was not only unnecessary to do so, but not the thing. However, there were the other visits to be got through. It was the first two on the list—those marked as to be paid "Without Fail"—that most alarmed me. Prince Ivan Ivanovitch was a commander-in-chief, as well as old, wealthy, and a bachelor. Consequently, I foresaw that vis-a-vis conversation between him and myself—myself a sixteen-year-old student!—was not likely to be interesting. As for the Iwins, they too were rich—the father being a departmental official of high rank who had only on one occasion called at our house during my grandmother's time. Since her death, I had remarked that the younger Iwin had fought shy of us, and seemed to give himself airs. The elder of the pair, I had heard, had now finished his course in jurisprudence, and gone to hold a post in St. Petersburg, while his brother Sergius (the former object of my worship) was also in St. Petersburg, as a great fat cadet in the Corps of Pages.

When I was a young man, not only did I dislike intercourse with people who thought themselves above me, but such intercourse was, for me, an unbearable torture, owing partly to my constant dread of being snubbed, and partly to my straining every faculty of my intellect to prove to such people my independence. Yet, even if I failed to fulfil the latter part of my father's instructions, I felt that I must carry out the former. I paced my room and eyed my clothes ready disposed on chairs—the tunic, the sword, and the cap. Just as I was about to set forth, old Grap called to congratulate me, bringing with him Ilinka. Grap pere was a Russianised German and an intolerably effusive, sycophantic old man who was more often than not tipsy. As a rule, he visited us only when he wanted to ask for something, and although Papa sometimes entertained him in his study, old Grap never came to dinner with us. With his subserviency and begging propensities went such a faculty of good-humour and a power of making himself at home that every one looked upon his attachment to us as a great honour. For my part, however, I never liked him, and felt ashamed when he was speaking.

I was much put out by the arrival of these visitors, and made no effort to conceal the fact. Upon Ilinka I had been so used to look down, and he so used to recognise my right to do so, that it displeased me to think that he was now as much a matriculated student as myself. In some way he appeared to me to have made a POINT of attaining that equality. I greeted the pair coldly, and, without offering them any refreshment (since it went against the grain to do so, and I thought they could ask for anything, if they wanted it, without my first inviting them to state their requirements), gave orders for the drozhki to be got ready. Ilinka was a good-natured, extremely moral, and far from stupid young fellow; yet, for all that, what people call a person of moods. That is to say, for no apparent reason he was for ever in some PRONOUNCED frame of mind—now lachrymose, now frivolous, now touchy on the very smallest point. At the present moment he appeared to be in the last-named mood. He kept looking from his father to myself without speaking, except when directly addressed, at which times he smiled the self-deprecatory, forced smile under which he was accustomed to conceal his feelings, and more especially that feeling of shame for his father which he must have experienced in our house.

"So, Nicolas Petrovitch," the old man said to me, following me everywhere about the room as I went through the operation of dressing, while all the while his fat fingers kept turning over and over a silver snuff-box with which my grandmother had once presented me, "as soon as ever I heard from my son that you had passed your examinations so well (though of course your abilities are well-known to everyone), I at once came to congratulate you, my dear boy. Why, I have carried you on my shoulders before now, and God knows that I love you as though you were my own son. My Ilinka too has always been fond of you, and feels quite at home with you."

Meanwhile the said Ilinka remained sitting silently by the window, apparently absorbed in contemplation of my three-cornered cap, and every now and then angrily muttering something in an undertone.

"Now, I also wanted to ask you, Nicolas Petrovitch." His father went on, "whether my son did well in the examinations? He tells me that he is going to be in the same faculty as yourself, and that therefore you will be able to keep an eye on him, and advise him, and so on."

"Oh, yes, I suppose he passed well," I replied, with a glance at Ilinka, who, conscious of my gaze, reddened violently and ceased to move his lips about. "And might he spend the day with you?" was the father's next request, which he made with a deprecatory smile, as though he stood in actual awe of me, yet always keeping so close to me, wherever I moved, that the fumes of the drink and tobacco in which he had been indulging were constantly perceptible to my nostrils. I felt greatly vexed at his placing me in such a false position towards his son, as well as at his distracting my attention from what was, to me, a highly important operation—namely, the operation of dressing; while, over and above all, I was annoyed by the smell of liquor with which he followed me about. Accordingly, I said very coldly that I could not have the pleasure of Ilinka's company that day, since I should be out.

"Ah! I suppose you are going to see your sister?" put in Ilinka with a smile, but without looking at me. "Well, I too have business to attend to." At this I felt even more put out, as well as pricked with compunction; so, to soften my refusal a little, I hastened to say that the reason why I should not be at home that day was that I had to call upon the PRINCE Ivan Ivanovitch, the PRINCESS Kornakoff, and the Monsieur Iwin who held such an influential post, as well as, probably, to dine with the PRINCESS Nechludoff (for I thought that, on learning what important folk I was in the habit of mixing with, the Graps would no longer think it worth while to pretend to me). However, just as they were leaving, I invited Ilinka to come and see me another day; but he only murmured something unintelligible, and it was plain that he meant never to set foot in the house again.

When they had departed, I set off on my round of calls. Woloda, whom I had asked that morning to come with me, in order that I might not feel quite so shy as when altogether alone, had declined on the ground that for two brothers to be seen driving in one drozhki would appear so horribly "proper."

XVIII

The Valakhin Family

Accordingly I set off alone. My first call on the route lay at the Valakhin mansion. It was now three years since I had seen Sonetchka, and my love for her had long become a thing of the past, yet there still lingered in my heart a sort of clear, touching recollection of our bygone childish affection. At intervals, also, during those three years, I had found myself recalling her memory with such force and vividness that I had actually shed tears, and imagined myself to be in love with her again, but those occasions had not lasted more than a few minutes at a time, and had been long in recurring.

I knew that Sonetchka and her mother had been abroad—that, in fact, they had been so for the last two years. Also, I had heard that they had been in a carriage accident, and that Sonetchka's face had been so badly cut with the broken glass that her beauty was marred. As I drove to their house, I kept recalling the old Sonetchka to my mind, and wondering what she would look like when I met her. Somehow I imagined that, after her two years' sojourn abroad, she would look very tall, with a beautiful waist, and, though sedate and imposing, extremely attractive. Somehow, also, my imagination refused to picture her with her face disfigured with scars, but, on the contrary, since I had read somewhere of a lover who remained true to his adored one in spite of her disfigurement with smallpox, strove to imagine that I was in love with Sonetchka, for the purpose of priding myself on holding to my troth in spite of her scars—Yet, as a matter of fact, I was not really in love with her during that drive, but having once stirred up in myself old MEMORIES of love, felt PREPARED to fall into that condition, and the more so because, of late, my conscience had often been pricking me for having discarded so many of my old flames.

The Valakhins lived in a neat little wooden mansion approached by a courtyard. I gained admittance by ringing a bell (then a rarity in Moscow), and was received by a mincing, smartly-attired page. He either could not or made no attempt to inform me whether there was any one at home, but, leaving me alone in the dark hall, ran off down a still darker corridor. For a long time I waited in solitude in this gloomy place, out of which, in addition to the front door and the corridor, there only opened a door which at the moment was closed. Rather surprised at the dismal appearance of the house, I came to the conclusion that the reason was that its inmates were still abroad. After five minutes, however, the door leading into the salon was opened by the page boy, who then conducted me into a neat, but not richly furnished, drawing-room, where presently I was joined by Sonetchka.

She was now seventeen years old, and very small and thin, as well as of an unhealthy pallor of face. No scars at all were visible, however, and the beautiful, prominent eyes and bright, cheerful smile were the same as I had known and loved in my childhood. I had not expected her to look at all like this, and therefore could not at once lavish upon her the sentiment which I had been preparing on the way. She gave me her hand in the English fashion (which was then as much a novelty as a door-bell), and, bestowing upon mine a frank squeeze, sat down on the sofa by my side.

"Ah! how glad I am to see you, my dear Nicolas!" she said as she looked me in the face with an expression of pleasure so sincere that in the words "my dear Nicolas" I caught the purely friendly rather than the patronising note. To my surprise she seemed to me simpler, kinder, and more sisterly after her foreign tour than she had been before it. True, I could now see that she had two small scars between her nose and temples, but her wonderful eyes and smile fitted in exactly with my recollections, and shone as of old.

"But how greatly you have changed!" she went on. "You are quite grown-up now. And I-I-well, what do you think of me?"

"I should never have known you," I replied, despite the fact that at the moment I was thinking that I should have known her anywhere and always.

"Why? Am I grown so ugly?" she inquired with a movement of her head.

"Oh, no, decidedly not!" I hastened to reply. "But you have grown taller and older. As for being uglier, why, you are even—

"Yes, yes; never mind. Do you remember our dances and games, and St. Jerome, and Madame Dorat?" (As a matter of fact, I could not recollect any Madame Dorat, but saw that Sonetchka was being led away by the joy of her childish recollections, and mixing them up a little). "Ah! what a lovely time it was!" she went on—and once more there shone before me the same eyes and smile as I had always carried in my memory. While she had been speaking, I had been thinking over my position at the present moment, and had come to the conclusion that I was in love with her. The instant, however, that I arrived at that result my careless, happy mood vanished, a mist seemed to arise before me which concealed even her eyes and smile, and, blushing hotly, I became tongue-tied and ill-at-ease.

"But times are different now," she went on with a sigh and a little lifting of her eyebrows. "Everything seems worse than it used to be, and ourselves too. Is it not so, Nicolas?"

I could return her no answer, but sat silently looking at her.

"Where are those Iwins and Kornakoffs now? Do you remember them?" she continued, looking, I think, with some curiosity at my blushing, downcast countenance. "What splendid times we used to have!"

Still I could not answer her.

The next moment, I was relieved from this awkward position by the entry of old Madame Valakhin into the room. Rising, I bowed, and straightway recovered my faculty of speech. On the other hand, an extraordinary change now took place in Sonetchka. All her gaiety and bonhomie disappeared, her smile became quite a different one, and, except for the point of her shortness of stature, she became just the lady from abroad whom I had expected to find in her. Yet for this change there was no apparent reason, since her mother smiled every whit as pleasantly, and expressed in her every movement just the same benignity, as of old. Seating herself in her arm-chair, the old lady signed to me to come and sit beside her; after which she said something to her daughter in English, and Sonetchka left the room—a fact which still further helped to relieve me. Madame then inquired after my father and brother, and passed on to speak of her great bereavement—the loss of her husband. Presently, however, she seemed to become sensible of the fact that I was not helping much in the conversation, for she gave me a look as much as to say: "If, now, my dear boy, you were to get up, to take your leave, and to depart, it would be well." But a curious circumstance had overtaken me. While she had been speaking of her bereavement, I had recalled to myself, not only the fact that I was in love, but the probability that the mother knew of it: whereupon such a fit of bashfulness had come upon me that I felt powerless to put any member of my body to its legitimate use. I knew that if I were to rise and walk I should have to think where to plant each foot, what to do with my head, what with my hands, and so on. In a word, I foresaw that I should be very much as I had been on the night when I partook too freely of champagne, and therefore, since I felt uncertain of being able to manage myself if I DID rise, I ended by feeling UNABLE to rise. Meanwhile, I should say, Sonetchka had returned to the room with her work, and seated herself in a far corner—a corner whence, as I was nevertheless sensible, she could observe me. Madame must have felt some surprise as she gazed at my crimson face and noted my complete immobility, but I decided that it was better to continue sitting in that absurd position than to risk something unpleasant by getting up and walking. Thus I sat on and on, in the hope that some unforeseen chance would deliver me from my predicament. That unforeseen chance at length presented itself in the person of an unforeseen young man, who entered the room with an air of being one of the household, and bowed to me politely as he did so: whereupon Madame rose, excused herself to me for having to speak with her "homme d'affaires," and finally gave me a glance which said: "Well, if you DO mean to go on sitting there for ever, at least I can't drive you away." Accordingly, with a great effort I also rose, but, finding it impossible to do any leave-taking, moved away towards the door, followed by the pitying glances of mother and daughter. All at once I stumbled over a chair, although it was lying quite out of my route: the reason for my stumbling being that my whole attention was centred upon not tripping over the carpet. Driving through the fresh air, however—where at first I muttered and fidgeted about so much that Kuzma, my coachman, asked me what was the matter—I soon found this feeling pass away, and began to meditate quietly concerning my love for Sonetchka and her relations with her mother, which had appeared to me rather strange. When, afterwards, I told my father that mother and daughter had not seemed on the best of terms with one another, he said:

"Yes, Madame leads the poor girl an awful life with her meanness. Yet," added my father with a greater display of feeling than a man might naturally conceive for a mere relative, "she used to be such an original, dear, charming woman! I cannot think what has made her change so much. By the way, you didn't notice a secretary fellow about, did you? Fancy a Russian lady having an affaire with a secretary!"

"Yes, I saw him," I replied.

"And was he at least good-looking?"

"No, not at all."

"It is extraordinary!" concluded Papa, with a cough and an irritable hoist of his shoulder.

"Well, I am in love!" was my secret thought to myself as I drove along in my drozhki.

XIX

The Kornakoffs

My second call on the route lay at the Kornakoffs', who lived on the first floor of a large mansion facing the Arbat. The staircase of the building looked extremely neat and orderly, yet in no way luxurious—being lined only with drugget pinned down with highly-polished brass rods. Nowhere were there any flowers or mirrors to be seen. The salon, too, with its polished floor, which I traversed on my way to the drawing-room, was decorated in the same cold, severe, unostentatious style. Everything in it looked bright and solid, but not new, and pictures, flower-stands, and articles of bric-a-brac were wholly absent. In the drawing-room I found some of the young princesses seated, but seated with the sort of correct, "company" air about them which gave one the impression that they sat like that only when guests were expected.

"Mamma will be here presently," the eldest of them said to me as she seated herself by my side. For the next quarter of an hour, this young lady entertained me with such an easy flow of small-talk that the conversation never flagged a moment. Yet somehow she made so patent the fact that she was just entertaining me that I felt not altogether pleased. Amongst other things, she told me that their brother Stephen (whom they called Etienne, and who had been two years at the College of Cadets) had now received his commission. Whenever she spoke of him, and more particularly when she told me that he had flouted his mother's wishes by entering the Hussars, she assumed a nervous air, and immediately her sisters, sitting there in silence, also assumed a nervous air. When, again, she spoke of my grandmother's death, she assumed a MOURNFUL air, and immediately the others all did the same. Finally, when she recalled how I had once struck St. Jerome and been expelled from the room, she laughed and showed her bad teeth, and immediately all the other princesses laughed and showed their bad teeth too.

Next, the Princess-Mother herself entered—a little dried-up woman, with a wandering glance and a habit of always looking at somebody else when she was addressing one. Taking my hand, she raised her own to my lips for me to kiss it—which otherwise, not supposing it to be necessary, I should not have done.

"How pleased I am to see you!" she said with her usual clearness of articulation as she gazed at her daughters. "And how like your mother you look! Does he not, Lise?"

Lise assented, though I knew for a fact that I did not resemble my mother in the least.

"And what a grown-up you have become! My Etienne, you will remember, is your second cousin. No, not second cousin—what is it, Lise? My mother was Barbara Dimitrievna, daughter of Dimitri Nicolaevitch, and your grandmother was Natalia Nicolaevna."

"Then he is our THIRD cousin, Mamma," said the eldest girl.

"Oh, how you always confuse me!" was her mother's angry reply. "Not third cousin, but COUSIN GERMAN—that is your relationship to Etienne. He is an officer now. Did you know it? It is not well that he should have his own way too much. You young men need keeping in hand, or—! Well, you are not vexed because your old aunt tells you the plain truth? I always kept Etienne strictly in hand, for I found it necessary to do so."

"Yes, that is how our relationship stands," she went on. "Prince Ivan Ivanovitch is my uncle, and your late mother's uncle also. Consequently I must have been your mother's first cousin—no, second cousin. Yes, that is it. Tell me, have you been to call on Prince Ivan yet?"

I said no, but that I was just going to.

"Ah, is it possible?" she cried. "Why, you ought to have paid him the first call of all! Surely you know that he stands to you in the position of a father? He has no children of his own, and his only heirs are yourself and my children. You ought to pay him all possible deference, both because of his age, and because of his position in the world, and because of everything else. I know that you young fellows of the present day think nothing of relationships and are not fond of old men, yet do you listen to me, your old aunt, for I am fond of you, and was fond of your mother, and had a great—a very great-liking and respect for your grandmother. You must not fail to call upon him on any account."

I said that I would certainly go, and since my present call seemed to me to have lasted long enough, I rose, and was about to depart, but she restrained me.

"No, wait a minute," she cried. "Where is your father, Lise? Go and tell him to come here. He will be so glad to see you," she added, turning to me.

Two minutes later Prince Michael entered. He was a short, thick-set gentleman, very slovenly dressed and ill-shaven, yet wearing such an air of indifference that he looked almost a fool. He was not in the least glad to see me—at all events he did not intimate that he was; but the Princess (who appeared to stand in considerable awe of him) hastened to say:

"Is not Woldemar here" (she seemed to have forgotten my name) "exactly like his mother?" and she gave her husband a glance which forced him to guess what she wanted. Accordingly he approached me with his usual passionless, half-discontented expression, and held out to me an unshaven cheek to kiss.

"Why, you are not dressed yet, though you have to go out soon!" was the Princess's next remark to him in the angry tone which she habitually employed in conversation with her domestics. "It will only mean your offending some one again, and trying to set people against you."

"In a moment, in a moment, mother," said Prince Michael, and departed. I also made my bows and departed.

This was the first time I had heard of our being related to Prince Ivan Ivanovitch, and the news struck me unpleasantly.

XX

THE IWINS

As for the prospect of my call upon the Prince, it seemed even more unpleasant. However, the order of my route took me first to the Iwins, who lived in a large and splendid mansion in Tverskaia Street. It was not without some nervousness that I entered the great portico where a Swiss major-domo stood armed with his staff of office.

To my inquiry as to whether any one was at home he replied: "Whom do you wish to see, sir? The General's son is within."

"And the General himself?" I asked with forced assurance.

"I must report to him your business first. What may it be, sir?" said the major-domo as he rang a bell. Immediately the gaitered legs of a footman showed themselves on the staircase above; whereupon I was seized with such a fit of nervousness that I hastily bid the lacquey say nothing about my presence to the General, since I would first see his son. By the time I had reached the top of the long staircase, I seemed to have grown extremely small (metaphorically, I mean, not actually), and had very much the same feeling within me as had possessed my soul when my drozhki drew up to the great portico, namely, a feeling as though drozhki, horse, and coachman had all of them grown extremely small too. I found the General's son lying asleep on a sofa, with an open book before him. His tutor, Monsieur Frost, under whose care he still pursued his studies at home, had entered behind me with a sort of boyish tread, and now awoke his pupil. Iwin evinced no particular pleasure at seeing me, while I also seemed to notice that, while talking to me, he kept looking at my eyebrows. Although he was perfectly polite, I conceived that he was "entertaining" me much as the Princess Valakhin had done, and that he not only felt no particular liking for me, but even that he considered my acquaintance in no way necessary to one who possessed his own circle of friends. All this arose out of the idea that he was regarding my eyebrows. In short, his bearing towards me appeared to be (as I recognised with an awkward sensation) very much the same as my own towards Ilinka Grap. I began to feel irritated, and to interpret every fleeting glance which he cast at Monsieur Frost as a mute inquiry: "Why has this fellow come to see me?"

After some conversation he remarked that his father and mother were at home. Would I not like to visit them too?

"First I will go and dress myself," he added as he departed to another room, notwithstanding that he had seemed to be perfectly well dressed (in a new frockcoat and white waistcoat) in the present one. A few minutes later he reappeared in his University uniform, buttoned up to the chin, and we went downstairs together. The reception rooms through which we passed were lofty and of great size, and seemed to be richly furnished with marble and gilt ornaments, chintz-covered settees, and a number of mirrors. Presently Madame Iwin met us, and we went into a little room behind the drawing-room, where, welcoming me in very friendly fashion, she seated herself by my side, and began to inquire after my relations.

Closer acquaintance with Madame (whom I had seen only twice before, and that but for a moment on each occasion) impressed me favourably. She was tall, thin, and very pale, and looked as though she suffered from chronic depression and fatigue. Yet, though her smile was a sad one, it was very kind, and her large, mournful eyes, with a slight cast in their vision, added to the pathos and attractiveness of her expression. Her attitude, while not precisely that of a hunchback, made her whole form droop, while her every movement expressed languor. Likewise, though her speech was deliberate, the timbre of her voice, and the manner in which she lisped her r's and l's, were very pleasing to the ear. Finally, she did not "ENTERTAIN" me. Unfortunately, the answers which I returned to her questions concerning my relations seemed to afford her a painful interest, and to remind her of happier days: with the result that when, presently, her son left the room, she gazed at me in silence for a moment, and then burst into tears. As I sat there in mute bewilderment, I could not conceive what I had said to bring this about. At first I felt sorry for her as she sat there weeping with downcast eyes. Next I began to think to myself: "Ought I not to try and comfort her, and how ought that to be done?" Finally, I began to feel vexed with her for placing me in such an awkward position. "Surely my appearance is not so moving as all that?" I reflected. "Or is she merely acting like this to see what I shall do under the circumstances?"

"Yet it would not do for me to go," I continued to myself, "for that would look too much as though I were fleeing to escape her tears." Accordingly I began fidgeting about on my seat, in order to remind her of my presence.

"Oh, how foolish of me!" at length she said, as she gazed at me for a moment and tried to smile. "There are days when one weeps for no reason whatever." She felt about for her handkerchief, and then burst out weeping more violently than before.

"Oh dear! How silly of me to be for ever crying like this! Yet I was so fond of your mother! We were such friends! We-we—"

At this point she found her handkerchief, and, burying her face in it, went on crying. Once more I found myself in the same protracted dilemma. Though vexed, I felt sorry for her, since her tears appeared to be genuine—even though I also had an idea that it was not so much for my mother that she was weeping as for the fact that she was unhappy, and had known happier days. How it would all have ended I do not know, had not her son reappeared and said that his father desired to see her. Thereupon she rose, and was just about to leave the room, when the General himself entered. He was a small, grizzled, thick-set man, with bushy black eyebrows, a grey, close-cropped head, and a very stern, haughty expression of countenance.

I rose and bowed to him, but the General (who was wearing three stars on his green frockcoat) not only made no response to my salutation, but scarcely even looked at me; so that all at once I felt as though I were not a human being at all, but only some negligible object such as a settee or window; or, if I were a human being, as though I were quite indistinguishable from such a negligible object.

"Then you have not yet written to the Countess, my dear?" he said to his wife in French, and with an imperturbable, yet determined, expression on his countenance.

"Good-bye, Monsieur Irtenieff," Madame said to me, in her turn, as she made a proud gesture with her head and looked at my eyebrows just as her son had done. I bowed to her, and again to her husband, but my second salutation made no more impression upon him than if a window had just been opened or closed. Nevertheless the younger Iwin accompanied me to the door, and on the way told me that he was to go to St. Petersburg University, since his father had been appointed to a post in that city (and young Iwin named a very high office in the service).

"Well, his Papa may do whatsoever he likes," I muttered to myself as I climbed into the drozhki, "but at all events I will never set foot in that house again. His wife weeps and looks at me as though I were the embodiment of woe, while that old pig of a General does not even give me a bow. However, I will get even with him some day." How I meant to do that I do not know, but my words nevertheless came true.

Afterwards, I frequently found it necessary to remember the advice of my father when he said that I must cultivate the acquaintanceship of the Iwins, and not expect a man in the position of General Iwin to pay any attention to a boy like myself. But I had figured in that position long enough.

XXI

Prince Ivan Ivanovitch

Now for the last call—the visit to Nikitskaia Street," I said to Kuzma, and we started for Prince Ivan Ivanovitch's mansion.

Towards the end, a round of calls usually brings one a certain amount of self-assurance: consequently I was approaching the Prince's abode in quite a tranquil frame of mind, when suddenly I remembered the Princess Kornakoff's words that I was his heir, and at the same moment caught sight of two carriages waiting at the portico. Instantly, my former nervousness returned.

Both the old major-domo who opened the door to me, and the footman who took my coat, and the two male and three female visitors whom I found in the drawing-room, and, most of all, Prince Ivan Ivanovitch himself (whom I found clad in a "company" frockcoat and seated on a sofa) seemed to look at me as at an Heir, and so to eye me with ill-will. Yet the Prince was very gracious and, after kissing me (that is to say, after pressing his cold, dry, flabby lips to my cheek for a second), asked me about my plans and pursuits, jested with me, inquired whether I still wrote verses of the kind which I used to indite in honour of my grandmother's birthdays, and invited me to dine with him that day. Nevertheless, in proportion as he grew the kinder, the more did I feel persuaded that his civility was only intended to conceal from me the fact that he disliked the idea of my being his heir. He had a custom (due to his false teeth, of which his mouth possessed a complete set) of raising his upper lip a little as he spoke, and producing a slight whistling sound from it; and whenever, on the present occasion, he did so it seemed to me that he was saying to himself: "A boy, a boy—I know it! And my heir, too—my heir!"

When we were children, we had been used to calling the Prince "dear Uncle;" but now, in my capacity of heir, I could not bring my tongue to the phrase, while to say "Your Highness," as did one of the other visitors, seemed derogatory to my self-esteem. Consequently, never once during that visit did I call him anything at all. The personage, however, who most disturbed me was the old Princess who shared with me the position of prospective inheritor, and who lived in the Prince's house. While seated beside her at dinner, I felt firmly persuaded that the reason why she would not speak to me was that she disliked me for being her co-heir, and that the Prince, for his part, paid no attention to our side of the table for the reason that the Princess and myself hoped to succeed him, and so were alike distasteful in his sight.

"You cannot think how I hated it all!" I said to Dimitrieff the same evening, in a desire to make a parade of disliking the notion of being an heir (somehow I thought it the thing to do). "You cannot think how I loathed the whole two hours that I spent there!—Yet he is a fine-looking old fellow, and was very kind to me," I added—wishing, among other things, to disabuse my friend of any possible idea that my loathing had arisen out of the fact that I had felt so small. "It is only the idea that people may be classing me with the Princess who lives with him, and who licks the dust off his boots. He is a wonderful old man, and good and considerate to everybody, but it is awful to see how he treats the Princess. Money is a detestable thing, and ruins all human relations."

"Do you know, I think it would be far the best thing for me to have an open explanation with the Prince," I went on; "to tell him that I respect him as a man, but think nothing of being his heir, and that I desire him to leave me nothing, since that is the only condition on which I can, in future, visit his house."

Instead of bursting out laughing when I said this, Dimitri pondered awhile in silence, and then answered:

"You are wrong. Either you ought to refrain from supposing that people may be classing you with this Princess of whom you speak, or, if you Do suppose such a thing, you ought to suppose further that people are thinking what you yourself know quite well—namely, that such thoughts are so utterly foreign to your nature that you despise them and would never make them a basis for action. Suppose, however, that people Do suppose you to suppose such a thing—Well, to sum up," he added, feeling that he was getting a little mixed in his pronouncements, "you had much better not suppose anything of the kind."

My friend was perfectly right, though it was not until long, long afterwards that experience of life taught me the evil that comes of thinking—still worse, of saying—much that seems very fine; taught me that there are certain thoughts which should always be kept to oneself, since brave words seldom go with brave deeds. I learnt then that the mere fact of giving utterance to a good intention often makes it difficult, nay, impossible, to carry that good intention into effect. Yet how is one to refrain from giving utterance to the brave, self-sufficient impulses of youth? Only long afterwards does one remember and regret them, even as one incontinently plucks a flower before its blooming, and subsequently finds it lying crushed and withered on the ground.

The very next morning I, who had just been telling my friend Dimitri that money corrupts all human relations, and had (as we have seen) squandered the whole of my cash on pictures and Turkish pipes, accepted a loan of twenty roubles which he suggested should pay for my travelling expenses into the country, and remained a long while thereafter in his debt!

XXII

Intimate Conversation With My Friend

This conversation of ours took place in a phaeton on the way to Kuntsevo. Dimitri had invited me in the morning to go with him to his mother's, and had called for me after luncheon; the idea being that I should spend the evening, and perhaps also pass the night, at the country-house where his family lived. Only when we had left the city and exchanged its grimy streets and the unbearably deafening clatter of its pavements for the open vista of fields and the subdued grinding of carriage-wheels on a dusty high road (while the sweet spring air and prospect enveloped us on every side) did I awake from the new impressions and sensations of freedom into which the past two days had plunged me. Dimitri was in his kind and sociable mood. That is to say, he was neither frowning nor blinking nervously nor straightening his neck in his collar. For my own part, I was congratulating myself on those noble sentiments which I have expressed above, in the belief that they had led him to overlook my shameful encounter with Kolpikoff, and to refrain from despising me for it. Thus we talked together on many an intimate subject which even a friend seldom mentions to a friend. He told me about his family whose acquaintance I had not yet made—about his mother, his aunt, and his sister, as also about her whom Woloda and Dubkoff believed to be his "flame," and always spoke of as "the lady with the chestnut locks." Of his mother he spoke with a certain cold and formal commendation, as though to forestall any further mention of her; his aunt he extolled enthusiastically, though with a touch of condescension in his tone; his sister he scarcely mentioned at all, as though averse to doing so in my presence; but on the subject of "the lady with the chestnut locks" (whose real name was Lubov Sergievna, and who was a grown-up young lady living on a family footing with the Nechludoffs) he discoursed with animation.

"Yes, she is a wonderful woman," he said with a conscious reddening of the face, yet looking me in the eyes with dogged temerity. "True, she is no longer young, and even rather elderly, as well as by no means good-looking; but as for loving a mere featherhead, a mere beauty— well, I never could understand that, for it is such a silly thing to do."

(Dimitri said this as though he had just discovered a most novel and extraordinary truth.) "I am certain, too, that such a soul, such a heart and principles, as are hers are not to be found elsewhere in the world of the present day." (I do not know whence he had derived the habit of saying that few good things were discoverable in the world of the present day, but at all events he loved to repeat the expression, and it somehow suited him.)

"Only, I am afraid," he went on quietly, after thus annihilating all such men as were foolish enough to admire mere beauty, "I am afraid that you will not understand or realise her quickly. She is modest, even secretive, and by no means fond of exhibiting her beautiful and surprising qualities. Now, my mother—who, as you will see, is a noble, sensible woman—has known Lubov Sergievna, for many years; yet even to this day she does not properly understand her. Shall I tell you why I was out of temper last evening when you were questioning me? Well, you must know that the day before yesterday Lubov asked me to accompany her to Ivan Yakovlevitch's (you have heard of him, I suppose? the fellow who seems to be mad, but who, in reality, is a very remarkable man). Well, Lubov is extremely religious, and understands Ivan Yakovlevitch to the full. She often goes to see him, and converses with him, and gives him money for the poor—money which she has earned herself. She is a marvellous woman, as you will see. Well, I went with her to Ivan's, and felt very grateful to her for having afforded me the opportunity of exchanging a word with so remarkable a man; but my mother could not understand our action at all, and discerned in it only superstition. Consequently, last night she and I quarrelled for the first time in our lives. A very bitter one it was, too," he concluded, with a convulsive shrug of his shoulders, as though the mention of it recalled the feelings which he had then experienced.

"And what are your intentions about it all?" I inquired, to divert him from such a disagreeable recollection. "That is to say, how do you imagine it is going to turn out? Do you ever speak to her about the future, or about how your love or friendship are going to end?"

"Do you mean, do I intend to marry her eventually?" he inquired, in his turn, with a renewed blush, but turning himself round and looking me boldly in the face.

"Yes, certainly," I replied as I settled myself down. "We are both of us grown-up, as well as friends, so we may as well discuss our future life as we drive along. No one could very well overlook or overhear us now."

"Why should I NOT marry her?" he went on in response to my reassuring reply. "It is my aim—as it should be the aim of every honourable man—to be as good and as happy as possible; and with her, if she should still be willing when I have become more independent, I should be happier and better than with the greatest beauty in the world."

Absorbed in such conversation, we hardly noticed that we were approaching Kuntsevo, or that the sky was becoming overcast and beginning to threaten rain. On the right, the sun was slowly sinking behind the ancient trees of the Kuntsevo park—one half of its brilliant disc obscured with grey, subluminous cloud, and the other half sending forth spokes of flaming light which threw the old trees into striking relief as they stood there with their dense crowns of green showing against a blue patch of sky. The light and shimmer of that patch contrasted sharply with the heavy pink cloud which lay massed above a young birch-tree visible on the horizon before us, while, a little further to the right, the parti-coloured roofs of the Kuntsevo mansion could be seen projecting above a belt of trees and undergrowth—one side of them reflecting the glittering rays of the sun, and the other side harmonising with the more louring portion of the heavens. Below us, and to the left, showed the still blue of a pond where it lay surrounded with pale-green laburnums—its dull, concave-looking depths repeating the trees in more sombre shades of colour over the surface of a hillock. Beyond the water spread the black expanse of a ploughed field, with the straight line of a dark-green ridge by which it was bisected running far into the distance, and there joining the leaden, threatening horizon.

On either side of the soft road along which the phaeton was pursuing the even tenour of its way, bright-green, tangled, juicy belts of rye were sprouting here and there into stalk. Not a motion was perceptible in the air, only a sweet freshness, and everything looked extraordinarily clear and bright. Near the road I could see a little brown path winding its way among the dark-green, quarter-grown stems of rye, and somehow that path reminded me vividly of our village, and somehow (through some connection of thought) the idea of that village reminded me vividly of Sonetchka, and so of the fact that I was in love with her.

Notwithstanding my fondness for Dimitri and the pleasure which his frankness had afforded me, I now felt as though I desired to hear no more about his feelings and intentions with regard to Lubov Sergievna, but to talk unstintedly about my own love for Sonetchka, who seemed to me an object of affection of a far higher order. Yet for some reason or another I could not make up my mind to tell him straight out how splendid it would seem when I had married Sonetchka and we were living in the country—of how we should have little children who would crawl about the floor and call me Papa, and of how delighted I should be when he, Dimitri, brought his wife, Lubov Sergievna, to see us, wearing an expensive gown. Accordingly, instead of saying all that, I pointed to the setting sun, and merely remarked: "Look, Dimitri! How splendid!"

To this, however, Dimitri made no reply, since he was evidently dissatisfied at my answering his confession (which it had cost him much to make) by directing his attention to natural objects (to which he was, in general, indifferent). Upon him Nature had an effect altogether different to what she had upon myself, for she affected him rather by her industry than by her beauty—he loved her rather with his intellect than with his senses.

"I am absolutely happy," I went on, without noticing that he was altogether taken up with his own thoughts and oblivious of anything that I might be saying. "You will remember how told you about a girl with whom I used to be in love when was a little boy? Well, I saw her again only this morning, and am now infatuated with her." Then I told him—despite his continued expression of indifference—about my love, and about all my plans for my future connubial happiness. Strangely enough, no sooner had I related in detail the whole strength of my feelings than I instantly became conscious of its diminution.

The rain overtook us just as we were turning into the avenue of birch-trees which led to the house, but it did not really wet us. I only knew that it was raining by the fact that I felt a drop fall, first on my nose, and then on my hand, and heard something begin to patter upon the young, viscous leaves of the birch-trees as, drooping their curly branches overhead, they seemed to imbibe the pure, shining drops with an avidity which filled the whole avenue with scent. We descended from the carriage, so as to reach the house the quicker through the garden, but found ourselves confronted at the entrance-door by four ladies, two of whom were knitting, one reading a book, and the fourth walking to and fro with a little dog. Thereupon, Dimitri began to present me to his mother, sister, and aunt, as well as to Lubov Sergievna. For a moment they remained where they were, but almost instantly the rain became heavier.

"Let us go into the verandah; you can present him to us there," said the lady whom I took to be Dimitri's mother, and we all of us ascended the entrance-steps.

XXIII

THE NECHLUDOFFS

From the first, the member of this company who struck me the most was Lubov Sergievna, who, holding a lapdog in her arms and wearing stout laced boots, was the last of the four ladies to ascend the staircase, and twice stopped to gaze at me intently and then kiss her little dog. She was anything but good-looking, since she was red-haired, thin, short, and slightly crooked. What made her plain face all the plainer was the queer way in which her hair was parted to one side (it looked like the wigs which bald women contrive for themselves). However much I should have liked to applaud my friend, I could not find a single comely feature in her. Even her brown eyes, though expressive of good-humour, were small and dull—were, in fact, anything but pretty; while her hands (those most characteristic of features), were though neither large nor ill-shaped, coarse and red.

As soon as we reached the verandah, each of the ladies, except Dimitri's sister Varenika—who also had been regarding me attentively out of her large, dark-grey eyes—said a few words to me before resuming her occupation, while Varenika herself began to read aloud from a book which she held on her lap and steadied with her finger.

The Princess Maria Ivanovna was a tall, well-built woman of forty. To judge by the curls of half-grey hair which descended below her cap one might have taken her for more, but as soon as ever one observed the fresh, extraordinarily tender, and almost wrinkleless face, as well as, most of all, the lively, cheerful sparkle of the large eyes, one involuntarily took her for less. Her eyes were black and very frank, her lips thin and slightly severe, her nose regular and slightly inclined to the left, and her hands ringless, large, and almost like those of a man, but with finely tapering fingers. She wore a dark-blue dress fastened to the throat and sitting closely to her firm, still youthful waist—a waist which she evidently pinched. Lastly, she held herself very upright, and was knitting a garment of some kind. As soon as I stepped on to the verandah she took me by the hand, drew me to her as though wishing to scrutinise me more closely, and said, as she gazed at me with the same cold, candid glance as her son's, that she had long known me by report from Dimitri, and that therefore, in order to make my acquaintance thoroughly, she had invited me to stay these twenty-four hours in her house.

"Do just as you please here," she said, "and stand on no ceremony whatever with us, even as we shall stand on none with you. Pray walk, read, listen, or sleep as the mood may take you."

Sophia Ivanovna was an old maid and the Princess's younger sister, though she looked the elder of the two. She had that exceedingly overstuffed appearance which old maids always present who are short of stature but wear corsets. It seemed as though her healthiness had shifted upwards to the point of choking her, her short, fat hands would not meet below her projecting bust, and the line of her waist was scarcely visible at all.

Notwithstanding that the Princess Maria Ivanovna had black hair and eyes, while Sophia Ivanovna had white hair and large, vivacious, tranquilly blue eyes (a rare combination), there was a great likeness between the two sisters, for they had the same expression, nose, and lips. The only difference was that Sophia's nose and lips were a trifle coarser than Maria's, and that, when she smiled, those features inclined towards the right, whereas Maria's inclined towards the left. Sophia, to judge by her dress and coiffure, was still youthful at heart, and would never have displayed grey curls, even if she had possessed them. Yet at first her glance and bearing towards me seemed very proud, and made me nervous, whereas I at once felt at home with the Princess. Perhaps it was only Sophia's stoutness and a certain resemblance to portraits of Catherine the Great that gave her, in my eyes, a haughty aspect, but at all events I felt quite intimidated when she looked at me intently and said, "Friends of our friends are our friends also." I became reassured and changed my opinion about her only when, after saying those words, she opened her mouth and sighed deeply. It may be that she owed her habit of sighing after every few words—with a great distention of the mouth and a slight drooping of her large blue eyes—to her stoutness, yet it was none the less one which expressed so much good-humour that I at once lost all fear of her, and found her actually attractive. Her eyes were charming, her voice pleasant and musical, and even the flowing lines of her fullness seemed to my youthful vision not wholly lacking in beauty.

I had imagined that Lubov Sergievna, as my friend's friend, would at once say something friendly and familiar to me; yet, after gazing at me fixedly for a while, as though in doubt whether the remark she was about to make to me would not be too friendly, she at length asked me what faculty I was in. After that she stared at me as before, in evident hesitation as to whether or not to say something civil and familiar, until, remarking her perplexity, I besought her with a look to speak freely. Yet all she then said was, "They tell me the Universities pay very little attention to science now," and turned away to call her little dog.

All that evening she spoke only in disjointed fragments of this kind—fragments which had no connection either with the point or with one another; yet I had such faith in Dimitri, and he so often kept looking from her to me with an expression which mutely asked me, "Now, what do you think of that?" that, though I entirely failed to persuade myself that in Lubov Sergievna there was anything to speak of, I could not bear to express the thought, even to myself.

As for the last member of the family, Varenika, she was a well-developed girl of sixteen. The only good features in her were a pair of dark-grey eyes,—which, in their expression of gaiety mingled with quiet attention, greatly resembled those of her aunt—a long coil of flaxen hair, and extremely delicate, beautiful hands.

"I expect, Monsieur Nicolas, you find it wearisome to hear a story begun from the middle?" said Sophia Ivanovna with her good-natured sigh as she turned over some pieces of clothing which she was sewing. The reading aloud had ceased for the moment because Dimitri had left the room on some errand or another.

"Or perhaps you have read Rob Roy before?" she added.

At that period I thought it incumbent upon me, in virtue of my student's uniform, to reply in a very "clever and original" manner to every question put to me by people whom I did not know very well, and regarded such short, clear answers as "Yes," "No," "I like it," or "I do not care for it," as things to be ashamed of. Accordingly, looking down at my new and fashionably-cut trousers and the glittering buttons of my tunic, I replied that I had never read Rob Roy, but that it interested me greatly to hear it, since I preferred to read books from the middle rather than from the beginning.

"It is twice as interesting," I added with a self-satisfied smirk; "for then one can guess what has gone before as well as what is to come after."

The Princess smiled what I thought was a forced smile, but one which I discovered later to be her only one.

"Well, perhaps that is true," she said. "But tell me, Nicolas (you will not be offended if I drop the Monsieur)—tell me, are you going to be in town long? When do you go away?"

"I do not know quite. Perhaps tomorrow, or perhaps not for some while yet," I replied for some reason or another, though I knew perfectly well that in reality we were to go tomorrow.

"I wish you could stop longer, both for your own sake and for Dimitri's," she said in a meditative manner. "At your age friendship is a weak thing."

I felt that every one was looking at me, and waiting to see what I should say—though certainly Varenika made a pretence of looking at her aunt's work. I felt, in fact, as though I were being put through an examination, and that it behoved me to figure in it as well as possible.

"Yes, to ME Dimitri's friendship is most useful," I replied, "but to HIM mine cannot be of any use at all, since he is a thousand times better than I" (Dimitri could not hear what I said, or I should have feared his detecting the insincerity of my words.)

Again the Princess smiled her unnatural, yet characteristically natural, smile.

"Just listen to him!" she said. "But it is YOU who are the little monster of perfection."

"'Monster of perfection,'" I thought to myself. "That is splendid. I must make a note of it."

"Yet, to dismiss yourself, he has been extraordinarily clever in that quarter," she went on in a lower tone (which pleased me somehow) as she indicated Lubov Sergievna with her eyes, "since he has discovered in our poor little Auntie" (such was the pet name which they gave Lubov) "all sorts of perfections which I, who have known her and her little dog for twenty years, had never yet suspected. Varenika, go and tell them to bring me a glass of water," she added, letting her eyes wander again. Probably she had bethought her that it was too soon, or not entirely necessary, to let me into all the family secrets. "Yet no—let HIM go, for he has nothing to do, while you are reading. Pray go to the door, my friend," she said to me, "and walk about fifteen steps down the passage. Then halt and call out pretty loudly, 'Peter, bring Maria Ivanovna a glass of iced water'"—and she smiled her curious smile once more.

"I expect she wants to say something about me in my absence," I thought to myself as I left the room. "I expect she wants to remark that she can see very clearly that I am a very, very clever young man."

Hardly had I taken a dozen steps when I was overtaken by Sophia Ivanovna, who, though fat and short of breath, trod with surprising lightness and agility.

"Merci, mon cher," she said. "I will go and tell them myself."

XXIV

LOVE

Sophia Ivanovna, as I afterwards came to know her, was one of those rare, young-old women who are born for family life, but to whom that happiness has been denied by fate. Consequently all that store of their love which should have been poured out upon a husband and children becomes pent up in their hearts, until they suddenly decide to let it overflow upon a few chosen individuals. Yet so inexhaustible is that store of old maids' love that, despite the number of individuals so selected, there still remains an abundant surplus of affection which they lavish upon all by whom they are surrounded—upon all, good or bad, whom they may chance to meet in their daily life.

Of love there are three kinds—love of beauty, the love which denies itself, and practical love.

Of the desire of a young man for a young woman, as well as of the reverse instance, I am not now speaking, for of such tendresses I am wary, seeing that I have been too unhappy in my life to have been able ever to see in such affection a single spark of truth, but rather a lying pretence in which sensuality, connubial relations, money, and the wish to bind hands or to unloose them have rendered feeling such a complex affair as to defy analysis. Rather am I speaking of that love for a human being which, according to the spiritual strength of its possessor, concentrates itself either upon a single individual, upon a few, or upon many—of love for a mother, a father, a brother, little children, a friend, a compatriot—of love, in short, for one's neighbour.

Love of beauty consists in a love of the sense of beauty and of its expression. People who thus love conceive the object of their affection to be desirable only in so far as it arouses in them that pleasurable sensation of which the consciousness and the expression soothes the senses. They change the object of their love frequently, since their principal aim consists in ensuring that the voluptuous feeling of their adoration shall be constantly titillated. To preserve in themselves this sensuous condition, they talk unceasingly, and in the most elegant terms, on the subject of the love which they feel, not only for its immediate object, but also for objects upon which it does not touch at all. This country of ours contains many such individuals—individuals of that well-known class who, cultivating "the beautiful," not only discourse of their cult to all and sundry, but speak of it pre-eminently in FRENCH. It may seem a strange and ridiculous thing to say, but I am convinced that among us we have had in the past, and still have, a large section of society—notably women—whose love for their friends, husbands, or children would expire tomorrow if they were debarred from dilating upon it in the tongue of France!

Love of the second kind—renunciatory love—consists in a yearning to undergo self-sacrifice for the object beloved, regardless of any consideration whether such self-sacrifice will benefit or injure the object in question. "There is no evil which I would not endure to show both the world and him or her whom I adore my devotion." There we have the formula of this kind of love. People who thus love never look for reciprocity of affection, since it is a finer thing to sacrifice yourself for one who does not comprehend you. Also, they are always painfully eager to exaggerate the merits of their sacrifice; usually constant in their love, for the reason that they would find it hard to forego the kudos of the deprivations which they endure for the object beloved; always ready to die, to prove to him or to her the entirety of their devotion; but sparing of such small daily proofs of their love as call for no special effort of self-immolation. They do not much care whether you eat well, sleep well, keep your spirits up, or enjoy good health, nor do they ever do anything to obtain for you those blessings if they have it in their power; but, should you be confronting a bullet, or have fallen into the water, or stand in danger of being burnt, or have had your heart broken in a love affair—well, for all these things they are prepared if the occasion should arise. Moreover, people addicted to love of such a self-sacrificing order are invariably proud of their love, exacting, jealous, distrustful, and—strange to tell—anxious that the object of their adoration should incur perils (so that they may save it from calamity, and console it thereafter) and even be vicious (so that they may purge it of its vice).

Suppose, now, that you are living in the country with a wife who loves you in this self-sacrificing manner. You may be healthy and contented, and have occupations which interest you, while, on the other hand, your wife may be too weak to superintend the household work (which, in consequence, will be left to the servants), or to look after the children (who, in consequence, will be left to the nurses), or to put her heart into any work whatsoever: and all because she loves nobody and nothing but yourself. She may be patently ill, yet she will say not a word to you about it, for fear of distressing you. She may be patently ennuyee, yet for your sake she will be prepared to be so for the rest of her life. She may be patently depressed because you stick so persistently to your occupations (whether sport, books, farming, state service, or anything else) and see clearly that they are doing you harm; yet, for all that, she will keep silence, and suffer it to be so. Yet, should you but fall sick—and, despite her own ailments and your prayers that she will not distress herself in vain, your loving wife will remain sitting inseparably by your bedside. Every moment you will feel her sympathetic gaze resting upon you and, as it were, saying: "There! I told you so, but it is all one to me, and I shall not leave you." In the morning you maybe a little better, and move into another room. The room, however, will be insufficiently warmed or set in order; the soup which alone you feel you could eat will not have been cooked; nor will any medicine have been sent for. Yet, though worn out with night watching, your loving wife will continue to regard you with an expression of sympathy, to walk about on tiptoe, and to whisper unaccustomed and obscure orders to the servants. You may wish to be read to—and your loving wife will tell you with a sigh that she feels sure you will be unable to hear her reading, and only grow angry at her awkwardness in doing it; wherefore you had better not be read to at all. You may wish to walk about the room—and she will tell you that it would be far better for you not to do so. You may wish to talk with some friends who have called—and she will tell you that talking is not good for you. At nightfall the fever may come upon you again, and you may wish to be left alone whereupon your loving wife, though wasted, pale, and full of yawns, will go on sitting in a chair opposite you, as dusk falls, until her very slightest movement, her very slightest sound, rouses you to feelings of anger and impatience. You may have a servant who has lived with you for twenty years, and to whom you are attached, and who would tend you well and to your satisfaction during the night, for the reason that he has been asleep all day and is, moreover, paid a salary for his services; yet your wife will not suffer him to wait upon you. No; everything she must do herself with her weak, unaccustomed fingers (of which you follow the movements with suppressed irritation as those pale members do their best to uncork a medicine bottle, to snuff a candle, to pour out physic, or to touch you in a squeamish sort of way). If you are an impatient, hasty sort of man, and beg of her to leave the room, you will hear by the vexed, distressed sounds which come from her that she is humbly sobbing and weeping behind the door, and whispering foolishness of some kind to the servant. Finally if you do not die, your loving wife—who has not slept during the whole three weeks of your illness (a fact of which she will constantly remind you)—will fall ill in her turn, waste away, suffer much, and become even more incapable of any useful pursuit than she was before; while by the time that you have regained your normal state of health she will express to you her self-sacrificing affection only by shedding around you a kind of benignant dullness which involuntarily communicates itself both to yourself and to every one else in your vicinity.

The third kind of love—practical love—consists of a yearning to satisfy every need, every desire, every caprice, nay, every vice, of the being beloved. People who love thus always love their life long, since, the more they love, the more they get to know the object beloved, and the easier they find the task of loving it—that is to say, of satisfying its desires. Their love seldom finds expression in words, but if it does so, it expresses itself neither with assurance nor beauty, but rather in a shamefaced, awkward manner, since people of this kind invariably have misgivings that they are loving unworthily. People of this kind love even the faults of their adored one, for the reason that those faults afford them the power of constantly satisfying new desires. They look for their affection to be returned, and even deceive themselves into believing that it is returned, and are happy accordingly: yet in the reverse case they will still continue to desire happiness for their beloved one, and try by every means in their power—whether moral or material, great or small—to provide it.

Such practical love it was—love for her nephew, for her niece, for her sister, for Lubov Sergievna, and even for myself, because I loved Dimitri—that shone in the eyes, as well as in the every word and movement, of Sophia Ivanovna.

Only long afterwards did I learn to value her at her true worth. Yet even now the question occurred to me: "What has made Dimitri—who throughout has tried to understand love differently to other young fellows, and has always had before his eyes the gentle, loving Sophia Ivanovna—suddenly fall so deeply in love with the incomprehensible Lubov Sergievna, and declare that in his aunt he can only find good QUALITIES? Verily it is a true saying that 'a prophet hath no honour in his own country.' One of two things: either every man has in him more of bad than of good, or every man is more receptive to bad than to good. Lubov Sergievna he has not known for long, whereas his aunt's love he has known since the day of his birth."

XXV

I Become Better Acquainted
with the Nechludoffs

When I returned to the verandah, I found that they were not talking of me at all, as I had anticipated. On the contrary, Varenika had laid aside the book, and was engaged in a heated dispute with Dimitri, who, for his part, was walking up and down the verandah, and frowningly adjusting his neck in his collar as he did so. The subject of the quarrel seemed to be Ivan Yakovlevitch and superstition, but it was too animated a difference for its underlying cause not to be something which concerned the family much more nearly. Although the Princess and Lubov Sergievna were sitting by in silence, they were following every word, and evidently tempted at times to take part in the dispute; yet always, just when they were about to speak, they checked themselves, and left the field clear for the two principles, Dimitri and Varenika. On my entry, the latter glanced at me with such an indifferent air that I could see she was wholly absorbed in the quarrel and did not care whether she spoke in my presence or not. The Princess too looked the same, and was clearly on Varenika's side, while Dimitri began, if anything, to raise his voice still more when I appeared, and Lubov Sergievna, for her part, observed to no one in particular: "Old people are quite right when they say, 'Si jeunesse savait, si vieillesse pouvait.'"

Nevertheless this quotation did not check the dispute, though it somehow gave me the impression that the side represented by the speaker and her friend was in the wrong. Although it was a little awkward for me to be present at a petty family difference, the fact that the true relations of the family revealed themselves during its progress, and that my presence did nothing to hinder that revelation, afforded me considerable gratification.

How often it happens that for years one sees a family cover themselves over with a conventional cloak of decorum, and preserve the real relations of its members a secret from every eye! How often, too, have I remarked that, the more impenetrable (and therefore the more decorous) is the cloak, the harsher are the relations which it conceals! Yet, once let some unexpected question—often a most trivial one (the colour of a woman's hair, a visit, a man's horses, and so forth)—arise in that family circle, and without any visible cause there will also arise an ever-growing difference, until in time the cloak of decorum becomes unequal to confining the quarrel within due bounds, and, to the dismay of the disputants and the astonishment of the auditors, the real and ill-adjusted relations of the family are laid bare, and the cloak, now useless for concealment, is bandied from hand to hand among the contending factions until it serves only to remind one of the years during which it successfully deceived one's perceptions. Sometimes to strike one's head violently against a ceiling hurts one less than just to graze some spot which has been hurt and bruised before: and in almost every family there exists some such raw and tender spot. In the Nechludoff family that spot was Dimitri's extraordinary affection for Lubov Sergievna, which aroused in the mother and sister, if not a jealous feeling, at all events a sense of hurt family pride. This was the grave significance which underlay, for all those present, the seeming dispute about Ivan Yakovlevitch and superstition.

"In anything that other people deride and despise you invariably profess to see something extraordinarily good!" Varenika was saying in her clear voice, as she articulated each syllable with careful precision.

"Indeed?" retorted Dimitri with an impatient toss of his head. "Now, in the first place, only a most unthinking person could ever speak of DESPISING such a remarkable man as Ivan Yakovlevitch, while, in the second place, it is YOU who invariably profess to see nothing good in what confronts you."

Meanwhile Sophia Ivanovna kept looking anxiously at us as she turned first to her nephew, and then to her niece, and then to myself. Twice she opened her mouth as though to say what was in her mind and drew a deep sigh.

"Varia, PLEASE go on reading," she said at length, at the same time handing her niece the book, and patting her hand kindly. "I wish to know whether he ever found HER again" (as a matter of fact, the novel in question contained not a word about any one finding any one else). "And, Mitia dear," she added to her nephew, despite the glum looks which he was throwing at her for having interrupted the logical thread of his deductions, "you had better let me poultice your cheek, or your teeth will begin to ache again."

After that the reading was resumed. Yet the quarrel had in no way dispelled the calm atmosphere of family and intellectual harmony which enveloped this circle of ladies.

LEO TOLSTOY

Clearly deriving its inspiration and character from the Princess Maria Ivanovna, it was a circle which, for me, had a wholly novel and attractive character of logicalness mingled with simplicity and refinement. That character I could discern in the daintiness, good taste, and solidity of everything about me, whether the handbell, the binding of the book, the settee, or the table. Likewise, I divined it in the upright, well-corseted pose of the Princess, in her pendant curls of grey hair, in the manner in which she had, at our first introduction, called me plain "Nicolas" and "he," in the occupations of the ladies (the reading and the sewing of garments), and in the unusual whiteness of their hands. Those hands, en passant, showed a family feature common to all—namely, the feature that the flesh of the palm on the outer side was rosy in colour, and divided by a sharp, straight line from the pure whiteness of the upper portion of the hand. Still more was the character of this feminine circle expressed in the manner in which the three ladies spoke Russian and French—spoke them, that is to say, with perfect articulation of syllables and pedantic accuracy of substantives and prepositions. All this, and more especially the fact that the ladies treated me as simply and as seriously as a real grown-up—telling me their opinions, and listening to my own (a thing to which I was so little accustomed that, for all my glittering buttons and blue facings, I was in constant fear of being told: "Surely you do not think that we are talking SERIOUSLY to you? Go away and learn something")—all this, I say, caused me to feel an entire absence of restraint in this society. I ventured at times to rise, to move about, and to talk boldly to each of the ladies except Varenika (whom I always felt it was unbecoming, or even forbidden, for me to address unless she first spoke to me).

As I listened to her clear, pleasant voice reading aloud, I kept glancing from her to the path of the flower-garden, where the rain-spots were making small dark circles in the sand, and thence to the lime-trees, upon the leaves of which the rain was pattering down in large detached drops shed from the pale, shimmering edge of the livid blue cloud which hung suspended over us. Then I would glance at her again, and then at the last purple rays of the setting sun where they were throwing the dense clusters of old, rain-washed birches into brilliant relief. Yet again my eyes would return to Varenika, and, each time that they did so, it struck me afresh that she was not nearly so plain as at first I had thought her.

"How I wish that I wasn't in love already!" I reflected, "or that Sonetchka was Varenika! How nice it would be if suddenly I could become a member of this family, and have the three ladies for my mother, aunt, and wife respectively!" All the time that these thoughts kept passing through my head I kept attentively regarding Varenika as she read, until somehow I felt as though I were magnetising her, and that presently she must look at me. Sure enough, at length she raised her head, threw me a glance, and, meeting my eyes, turned away.

"The rain does not seem to stop," she remarked.

Suddenly a new feeling came over me. I began to feel as though everything now happening to me was a repetition of some similar occurrence before—as though on some previous occasion a shower of rain had begun to fall, and the sun had set behind birch-trees, and I had been looking at her, and she had been reading aloud, and I had magnetised her, and she had looked up at me. Yes, all this I seemed to recall as though it had happened once before.

"Surely she is not—SHE?" was my thought. "Surely IT is not beginning?" However, I soon decided that Varenika was not the "SHE" referred to, and that "it" was not "beginning." "In the first place," I said to myself, "Varenika is not at all BEAUTIFUL. She is just an ordinary girl whose acquaintance I have made in the ordinary way, whereas the she whom I shall meet somewhere and some day and in some not ordinary way will be anything but ordinary. This family pleases me so much only because hitherto I have never seen anybody. Such things will always be happening in the future, and I shall see many more such families during my life."

XXVI

I Show Off

At tea time the reading came to an end, and the ladies began to talk among themselves of persons and things unknown to me. This I conceived them to be doing on purpose to make me conscious (for all their kind demeanour) of the difference which years and position in the world had set between them and myself. In general discussions, however, in which I could take part I sought to atone for my late silence by exhibiting that extraordinary cleverness and originality to which I felt compelled by my University uniform. For instance, when the conversation turned upon country houses, I said that Prince Ivan Ivanovitch had a villa near Moscow which people came to see even from London and Paris, and that it contained balustrading which had cost 380,000 roubles. Likewise, I remarked that the Prince was a very near relation of mine, and that, when lunching with him the same day, he had invited me to go and spend the entire summer with him at that villa, but that I had declined, since I knew the villa well, and had stayed in it more than once, and that all those balustradings and bridges did not interest me, since I could not bear ornamental work, especially in the country, where I liked everything to be wholly countrified. After delivering myself of this extraordinary and complicated romance, I grew confused, and blushed so much that every one must have seen that I was lying. Both Varenika, who was handing me a cup of tea, and Sophia Ivanovna, who had been gazing at me throughout, turned their heads away, and began to talk of something else with an expression which I afterwards learnt that good-natured people assume when a very young man has told them a manifest string of lies—an expression which says, "Yes, we know he is lying, and why he is doing it, the poor young fellow!"

What I had said about Prince Ivan Ivanovitch having a country villa, I had related simply because I could find no other pretext for mentioning both my relationship to the Prince and the fact that I had been to luncheon with him that day; yet why I had said all I had about the balustrading costing 380,000 roubles, and about my having several times visited the Prince at that villa (I had never once been there—more especially since the Prince possessed no residences save in Moscow and Naples, as the Nechludoffs very well knew), I could not possibly tell you. Neither in childhood nor in adolescence nor in riper years did I ever remark in myself the vice of falsehood—on the contrary, I was, if anything, too outspoken and truthful. Yet, during this first stage of my manhood, I often found myself seized with a strange and unreasonable tendency to lie in the most desperate fashion. I say advisedly "in the most desperate fashion," for the reason that I lied in matters in which it was the easiest thing in the world to detect me. On the whole I think that a vain-glorious desire to appear different from what I was, combined with an impossible hope that the lie would never be found out, was the chief cause of this extraordinary impulse.

After tea, since the rain had stopped and the after-glow of sunset was calm and clear, the Princess proposed that we should go and stroll in the lower garden, and admire her favourite spots there. Following my rule to be always original, and conceiving that clever people like myself and the Princess must surely be above the banalities of politeness, I replied that I could not bear a walk with no object in view, and that, if I Did walk, I liked to walk alone. I had no idea that this speech was simply rude; all I thought was that, even as nothing could be more futile than empty compliments, so nothing could be more pleasing and original than a little frank brusquerie. However, though much pleased with my answer, I set out with the rest of the company.

The Princess's favourite spot of all was at the very bottom of the lower garden, where a little bridge spanned a narrow piece of swamp. The view there was very restricted, yet very intimate and pleasing. We are so accustomed to confound art with nature that, often enough, phenomena of nature which are never to be met with in pictures seem to us unreal, and give us the impression that nature is unnatural, or vice versa; whereas phenomena of nature which occur with too much frequency in pictures seem to us hackneyed, and views which are to be met with in real life, but which appear to us too penetrated with a single idea or a single sentiment, seem to us arabesques. The view from the Princess's favourite spot was as follows. On the further side of a small lake, over-grown with weeds round its edges, rose a steep ascent covered with bushes and with huge old trees of many shades of green, while, overhanging the lake at the foot of the ascent, stood an ancient birch tree which, though partly supported by stout roots implanted in the marshy bank of the lake, rested its crown upon a tall, straight poplar, and dangled its curved branches over the smooth surface of the pond—

both branches and the surrounding greenery being reflected therein as in a mirror.

"How lovely!" said the Princess with a nod of her head, and addressing no one in particular.

"Yes, marvellous!" I replied in my desire to show that had an opinion of my own on every subject. "Yet somehow it all looks to me so terribly like a scheme of decoration."

The Princess went on gazing at the scene as though she had not heard me, and turning to her sister and Lubov Sergievna at intervals, in order to point out to them its details—especially a curved, pendent bough, with its reflection in the water, which particularly pleased her. Sophia Ivanovna observed to me that it was all very beautiful, and that she and her sister would sometimes spend hours together at this spot; yet it was clear that her remarks were meant merely to please the Princess. I have noticed that people who are gifted with the faculty of loving are seldom receptive to the beauties of nature. Lubov Sergievna also seemed enraptured, and asked (among other things), "How does that birch tree manage to support itself? Has it stood there long?" Yet the next moment she became absorbed in contemplation of her little dog Susetka, which, with its stumpy paws pattering to and fro upon the bridge in a mincing fashion, seemed to say by the expression of its face that this was the first time it had ever found itself out of doors. As for Dimitri, he fell to discoursing very logically to his mother on the subject of how no view can be beautiful of which the horizon is limited. Varenika alone said nothing. Glancing at her, I saw that she was leaning over the parapet of the bridge, her profile turned towards me, and gazing straight in front of her. Something seemed to be interesting her deeply, or even affecting her, since it was clear that she was oblivious to her surroundings, and thinking neither of herself nor of the fact that any one might be regarding her. In the expression of her large eyes there was nothing but wrapt attention and quiet, concentrated thought, while her whole attitude seemed so unconstrained and, for all her shortness, so dignified that once more some recollection or another touched me and once more I asked myself, "Is It, then, beginning?" Yet again I assured myself that I was already in love with Sonetchka, and that Varenika was only an ordinary girl, the sister of my friend. Though she pleased me at that moment, I somehow felt a vague desire to show her, by word or deed, some small unfriendliness.

"I tell you what, Dimitri," I said to my friend as I moved nearer to Varenika, so that she might overhear what I was going to say, "it seems to me that, even if there had been no mosquitos here, there would have been nothing to commend this spot; whereas"—and here I slapped my cheek, and in very truth annihilated one of those insects—"it is simply awful."

"Then you do not care for nature?" said Varenika without turning her head.

"I think it a foolish, futile pursuit," I replied, well satisfied that I had said something to annoy her, as well as something original. Varenika only raised her eyebrows a little, with an expression of pity, and went on gazing in front of her as calmly as before.

I felt vexed with her. Yet, for all that, the rusty, paint-blistered parapet on which she was leaning, the way in which the dark waters of the pond reflected the drooping branch of the overhanging birch tree (it almost seemed to me as though branch and its reflection met), the rising odour of the swamp, the feeling of crushed mosquito on my cheek, and her absorbed look and statuesque pose—many times afterwards did these things recur with unexpected vividness to my recollection.

XXVII

DIMITRI

When we returned to the house from our stroll, Varenika declined to sing as she usually did in the evenings, and I was conceited enough to attribute this to my doing, in the belief that its reason lay in what I had said on the bridge. The Nechludoffs never had supper, and went to bed early, while tonight, since Dimitri had the toothache (as Sophia Ivanovna had foretold), he departed with me to his room even earlier than usual. Feeling that I had done all that was required of me by my blue collar and gilt buttons, and that every one was very pleased with me, I was in a gratified, complacent mood, while Dimitri, on the other hand, was rendered by his quarrel with his sister and the toothache both taciturn and gloomy. He sat down at the table, got out a couple of notebooks—a diary and the copy-book in which it was his custom every evening to inscribe the tasks performed by or awaiting him—and, continually frowning and touching his cheek with his hand, continued writing for a while.

"Oh, Do leave me alone!" he cried to the maid whom Sophia Ivanovna sent to ask him whether his teeth were still hurting him, and whether he would not like to have a poultice made. Then, saying that my bed would soon be ready for me and that he would be back presently, he departed to Lubov Sergievna's room.

"What a pity that Varenika is not good-looking and, in general, Sonetchka!" I reflected when I found myself alone. "How nice it would be if, after I have left the University, I could go to her and offer her my hand! I would say to her, 'Princess, though no longer young, and therefore unable to love passionately, I will cherish you as a dear sister. And you,' I would continue to her mother, 'I greatly respect; and you, Sophia Ivanovna, I value highly. Therefore say to me, Varenika (since I ask you to be my wife), just the simple and direct word YES.' And she would give me her hand, and I should press it, and say, 'Mine is a love which depends not upon words, but upon deeds.' And suppose," next came into my head, "that Dimitri should suddenly fall in love with Lubotshka (as Lubotshka has already done with him), and should desire to marry her? Then either one or the other of us would have to resign all thought of marriage. Well, it would be splendid, for in that case I should act thus. As soon as I had noticed how things were, I should make no remark, but go to Dimitri and say, 'It is no use, my friend, for you and I to conceal our feelings from one another. You know that my love for your sister will terminate only with my life. Yet I know all; and though you have deprived me of all hope, and have rendered me an unhappy man, so that Nicolas Irtenieff will have to bewail his misery for the rest of his existence, yet do you take my sister,' and I should lay his hand in Lubotshka's. Then he would say to me, 'No, not for all the world!' and I should reply, 'Prince Nechludoff, it is in vain for you to attempt to outdo me in nobility. Not in the whole world does there exist a more magnanimous being than Nicolas Irtenieff.' Then I should salute him and depart. In tears Dimitri and Lubotshka would pursue me, and entreat me to accept their sacrifice, and I should consent to do so, and, perhaps, be happy ever afterwards—if only I were in love with Varenika." These fancies tickled my imagination so pleasantly that I felt as though I should like to communicate them to my friend; yet, despite our mutual vow of frankness, I also felt as though I had not the physical energy to do so.

Dimitri returned from Lubov Sergievna's room with some toothache capsules which she had given him, yet in even greater pain, and therefore in even greater depression, than before. Evidently no bedroom had yet been prepared for me, for presently the boy who acted as Dimitri's valet arrived to ask him where I was to sleep.

"Oh, go to the devil!" cried Dimitri, stamping his foot. "Vasika, Vasika, Vasika!" he went on, the instant that the boy had left the room, with a gradual raising of his voice at each repetition. "Vasika, lay me out a bed on the floor."

"No, let ME sleep on the floor," I objected.

"Well, it is all one. Lie anywhere you like," continued Dimitri in the same angry tone. "Vasika, why don't you go and do what I tell you?"

Evidently Vasika did not understand what was demanded of him, for he remained where he was.

"What is the matter with you? Go and lay the bed, Vasika, I tell you!" shouted Dimitri, suddenly bursting into a sort of frenzy; yet Vasika still did not understand, but, blushing hotly, stood motionless.

"So you are determined to drive me mad, are you?"—and leaping from his chair and rushing upon the boy, Dimitri struck him on the head with the whole weight of his fist, until the boy rushed headlong from the room. Halting in the doorway, Dimitri glanced at me, and the expression of fury and pain which had sat for a moment on his countenance suddenly gave place to such a boyish, kindly, affectionate, yet ashamed, expression that I felt sorry for him, and reconsidered my intention of leaving him to himself. He said nothing, but for a long time paced the room in silence, occasionally glancing at me with the same deprecatory expression as before. Then he took his notebook from the table, wrote something in it, took off his jacket and folded it carefully, and, stepping into the corner where the ikon hung, knelt down and began to say his prayers, with his large white hands folded upon his breast. So long did he pray that Vasika had time to bring a mattress and spread it, under my whispered directions, on the floor. Indeed, I had undressed and laid myself down upon the mattress before Dimitri had finished. As I contemplated his slightly rounded back and the soles of his feet (which somehow seemed to stick out in my direction in a sort of repentant fashion whenever he made his obeisances), I felt that I liked him more than ever, and debated within myself whether or not I should tell him all I had been fancying concerning our respective sisters. When he had finished his prayers, he lay down upon the bed near me, and, propping himself upon his elbow, looked at me in silence, with a kindly, yet abashed, expression. Evidently he found it difficult to do this, yet meant thus to punish himself. Then I smiled and returned his gaze, and he smiled back at me.

"Why do you not tell me that my conduct has been abominable?" he said. "You have been thinking so, have you not?"

"Yes," I replied; and although it was something quite different which had been in my mind, it now seemed to me that that was what I had been thinking. "Yes, it was not right of you, nor should I have expected it of you." It pleased me particularly at that moment to call him by the familiar second person singular. "But how are your teeth now?" I added.

"Oh, much better. Nicolinka, my friend," he went on, and so feelingly that it sounded as though tears were standing in his eyes, "I know and feel that I am bad, but God sees how I try to be better, and how I entreat Him to make me so. Yet what am I to do with such an unfortunate, horrible nature as mine? What am I to do with it? I try to keep myself in hand and to rule myself, but suddenly it becomes impossible for me to do so—at all events, impossible for me to do so unaided. I need the help and support of some one. Now, there is Lubov Sergievna; SHE understands me, and could help me in this, and I know by my notebook that I have greatly improved in this respect during the past year. Ah, my dear Nicolinka"—he spoke with the most unusual and unwonted tenderness, and in a tone which had grown calmer now that he had made his confession—"how much the influence of a woman like Lubov could do for me! Think how good it would be for me if I could have a friend like her to live with when I have become independent! With her I should be another man."

And upon that Dimitri began to unfold to me his plans for marriage, for a life in the country, and for continual self-discipline.

"Yes, I will live in the country," he said, "and you shall come to see me when you have married Sonetchka. Our children shall play together. All this may seem to you stupid and ridiculous, yet it may very well come to pass."

"Yes, it very well may" I replied with a smile, yet thinking how much nicer it would be if I married his sister.

"I tell you what," he went on presently; "you only imagine yourself to be in love with Sonetchka, whereas I can see that it is all rubbish, and that you do not really know what love means."

I did not protest, for, in truth, I almost agreed with him, and for a while we lay without speaking.

"Probably you have noticed that I have been in my old bad humour today, and have had a nasty quarrel with Varia?" he resumed. "I felt bad about it afterwards—more particularly since it occurred in your presence. Although she thinks wrongly on some subjects, she is a splendid girl and very good, as you will soon recognise."

His quick transition from mention of my love affairs to praise of his sister pleased me extremely, and made me blush, but I nevertheless said nothing more about his sister, and we went on talking of other things.

Thus we chattered until the cocks had crowed twice. In fact, the pale dawn was already looking in at the window when at last Dimitri lay down upon his bed and put out the candle.

"Well, now for sleep," he said.

"Yes," I replied, "but—"

"But what?"

"Now nice it is to be alive in the daylight!"

"Yes, it Is a splendid thing!" he replied in a voice which, even in the darkness, enabled me to see the expression of his cheerful, kindly eyes and boyish smile.

XXVIII

In the Country

Next day Woloda and myself departed in a post-chaise for the country. Turning over various Moscow recollections in my head as we drove along, I suddenly recalled Sonetchka Valakhin—though not until evening, and when we had already covered five stages of the road. "It is a strange thing," I thought, "that I should be in love, and yet have forgotten all about it. I must start and think about her," and straightway I proceeded to do so, but only in the way that one thinks when travelling—that is to say, disconnectedly, though vividly. Thus I brought myself to such a condition that, for the first two days after our arrival home, I somehow considered it incumbent upon me always to appear sad and moody in the presence of the household, and especially before Katenka, whom I looked upon as a great connoisseur in matters of this kind, and to whom I threw out a hint of the condition in which my heart was situated. Yet, for all my attempts at dissimulation and assiduous adoption of such signs of love sickness as I had occasionally observed in other people, I only succeeded for two days (and that at intervals, and mostly towards evening) in reminding myself of the fact that I was in love, and finally, when I had settled down into the new rut of country life and pursuits, I forgot about my affection for Sonetchka altogether.

We arrived at Petrovskoe in the night time, and I was then so soundly asleep that I saw nothing of the house as we approached it, nor yet of the avenue of birch trees, nor yet of the household—all of whom had long ago betaken themselves to bed and to slumber. Only old hunchbacked Foka—bare-footed, clad in some sort of a woman's wadded nightdress, and carrying a candlestick—opened the door to us. As soon as he saw who we were, he trembled all over with joy, kissed us on the shoulders, hurriedly put on his felt slippers, and started to dress himself properly. I passed in a semi-waking condition through the porch and up the steps, but in the hall the lock of the door, the bars and bolts, the crooked boards of the flooring, the chest, the ancient candelabrum (splashed all over with grease as of old), the shadows thrown by the crooked, chill, recently-lighted stump of candle, the perennially dusty, unopened window behind which I remembered sorrel to have grown—all was so familiar, so full of memories, so intimate of aspect, so, as it were, knit together by a single idea, that I suddenly became conscious of a tenderness for this quiet old house. Involuntarily I asked myself, "How have we, the house and I, managed to remain apart so long?" and, hurrying from spot to spot, ran to see if all the other rooms were still the same. Yes, everything was unchanged, except that everything had become smaller and lower, and I myself taller, heavier, and more filled out. Yet, even as I was, the old house received me back into its arms, and aroused in me with every board, every window, every step of the stairs, and every sound the shadows of forms, feelings, and events of the happy but irrevocable past. When we entered our old night nursery, all my childish fears lurked once more in the darkness of the corners and doorway. When we passed into the drawing-room, I could feel the old calm motherly love diffusing itself from every object in the apartment. In the breakfast-room, the noisy, careless merriment of childhood seemed merely to be waiting to wake to life again. In the divannaia (whither Foka first conducted us, and where he had prepared our beds) everything—mirror, screen, old wooden ikon, the lumps on the walls covered with white paper—seemed to speak of suffering and of death and of what would never come back to us again.

We got into bed, and Foka, bidding us good-night, retired.

"It was in this room that Mamma died, was it not?" said Woloda.

I made no reply, but pretended to be asleep. If I had said anything I should have burst into tears. On awaking next morning, I beheld Papa sitting on Woloda's bed in his dressing gown and slippers and smoking a cigar. Leaping up with a merry hoist of the shoulders, he came over to me, slapped me on the back with his great hand, and presented me his cheek to press my lips to.

"Well done, Diplomat!" he said in his most kindly jesting tone as he looked at me with his small bright eyes. "Woloda tells me you have passed the examinations well for a youngster, and that is a splendid thing. Unless you start and play the fool, I shall have another fine little fellow in you. Thanks, my dear boy. Well, we will have a grand time of it here now, and in the winter, perhaps, we shall move to St. Petersburg. I only wish the hunting was not over yet, or I could have given you some amusement in THAT way. Can you shoot, Woldemar? However, whether there is any game or not, I will take you out some day. Next winter, if God pleases, we will move to St. Petersburg, and you shall meet people, and make friends, for you are now my two young grown-ups. I have been telling

Woldemar that you are just starting on your careers, whereas my day is ended. You are old enough now to walk by yourselves, but, whenever you wish to confide in me, pray do so, for I am no longer your nurse, but your friend. At least, I will be your friend and comrade and adviser as much as I can and more than that I cannot do. How does that fall in with your philosophy, eh, Koko? Well or ill, eh?"

Of course I said that it fell in with it entirely, and, indeed, I really thought so. That morning Papa had a particularly winning, bright, and happy expression on his face, and these new relations between us, as of equals and comrades, made me love him all the more.

"Now, tell me," he went on, "did you call upon all our kinsfolk and the Iwins? Did you see the old man, and what did he say to you? And did you go to Prince Ivan's?"

We continued talking so long that, before we were fully dressed, the sun had left the window of the divannaia, and Jakoff (the same old man who of yore had twirled his fingers behind his back and always repeated his words) had entered the room and reported to Papa that the carriage was ready.

"Where are you going to?" I asked Papa.

"Oh, I had forgotten all about it!" he replied, with a cough and the usual hoisting of his shoulder. "I promised to go and call upon Epifanova today. You remember Epifanova—'la belle Flamande'—don't you, who used to come and see your Mamma? They are nice people." And with a self-conscious shrug of his shoulders (so it appeared to me) Papa left the room.

During our conversation, Lubotshka had more than once come to the door and asked "Can I come in?" but Papa had always shouted to her that she could not do so, since we were not dressed yet.

"What rubbish!" she replied. "Why, I have seen you in your dressing-gown."

"Never mind; you cannot see your brothers without their inexpressibles," rejoined Papa. "If they each of them just go to the door, let that be enough for you. Now go. Even for them to SPEAK to you in such a neglige costume is unbecoming."

"How unbearable you are!" was Lubotshka's parting retort. "Well, at least hurry up and come down to the drawing-room, for Mimi wants to see them."

As soon as Papa had left the room, I hastened to array myself in my student's uniform, and to repair to the drawing-room.

Woloda, on the other hand, was in no hurry, but remained sitting on his bed and talking to Jakoff about the best places to find plover and snipe. As I have said, there was nothing in the world he so much feared as to be suspected of any affection for his father, brother, and sister; so that, to escape any expression of that feeling, he often fell into the other extreme, and affected a coldness which shocked people who did not comprehend its cause. In the hall, I collided with Papa, who was hurrying towards the carriage with short, rapid steps. He had a new and fashionable Moscow greatcoat on, and smelt of scent. On seeing me, he gave a cheerful nod, as much as to say, "Do you remark my splendour?" and once again I was struck with the happy expression of face which I had noted earlier in the morning.

The drawing-room looked the same lofty, bright room as of Yore, with its brown English piano, and its large open windows looking on to the green trees and yellowish-red paths of the garden. After kissing Mimi and Lubotshka, I was approaching Katenka for the same purpose when it suddenly struck me that it might be improper for me to salute her in that fashion. Accordingly I halted, silent and blushing. Katenka, for her part, was quite at her ease as she held out a white hand to me and congratulated me on my passing into the University. The same thing took place when Woloda entered the drawing-room and met Katenka. Indeed, it was something of a problem how, after being brought up together and seeing one another daily, we ought now, after this first separation, to meet again. Katenka had grown better-looking than any of us, yet Woloda seemed not at all confused as, with a slight bow to her, he crossed over to Lubotshka, made a jesting remark to her, and then departed somewhere on some solitary expedition.

XXIX

Relations Between the Girls and Ourselves

Of the girls Woloda took the strange view that, although he wished that they should have enough to eat, should sleep well, be well dressed, and avoid making such mistakes in French as would shame him before strangers, he would never admit that they could think or feel like human beings, still less that they could converse with him sensibly about anything. Whenever they addressed to him a serious question (a thing, by the way, which he always tried to avoid), such as asking his opinion on a novel or inquiring about his doings at the University, he invariably pulled a grimace, and either turned away without speaking or answered with some nonsensical French phrase—"Comme c'est tres jolie!" or the like. Or again, feigning to look serious and stolidly wise, he would say something absolutely meaningless and bearing no relation whatever to the question asked him, or else suddenly exclaim, with a look of pretended unconsciousness, the word bulku or poyechali or kapustu, (Respectively, "roll of butter," "away," and "cabbage.") or something of the kind; and when, afterwards, I happened to repeat these words to him as having been told me by Lubotshka or Katenka, he would always remark:

"Hm! So you actually care about talking to them? I can see you are a duffer still"—and one needed to see and near him to appreciate the profound, immutable contempt which echoed in this remark. He had been grown-up now two years, and was in love with every good-looking woman that he met; yet, despite the fact that he came in daily contact with Katenka (who during those two years had been wearing long dresses, and was growing prettier every day), the possibility of his falling in love with her never seemed to enter his head. Whether this proceeded from the fact that the prosaic recollections of childhood were still too fresh in his memory, or whether from the aversion which very young people feel for everything domestic, or whether from the common human weakness which, at a first encounter with anything fair and pretty, leads a man to say to himself, "Ah! I shall meet much more of the same kind during my life," but at all events Woloda had never yet looked upon Katenka with a man's eyes.

All that summer Woloda appeared to find things very wearisome—a fact which arose out of that contempt for us all which, as I have said, he made no effort to conceal. His expression of face seemed to be constantly saying, "Phew! how it bores me to have no one to speak to!" The first thing in the morning he would go out shooting, or sit reading a book in his room, and not dress until luncheon time. Indeed, if Papa was not at home, he would take his book into that meal, and go on reading it without addressing so much as a single word to any one of us, who felt, somehow, guilty in his presence. In the evening, too, he would stretch himself on a settee in the drawing-room, and either go to sleep, propped on his elbow, or tell us farcical stories—sometimes stories so improper as to make Mimi grow angry and blush, and ourselves die with laughter. At other times he would not condescend to address a single serious word to any member of the family except Papa or (occasionally) myself. Involuntarily I offended against his view of girls, seeing that I was not so afraid of seeming affectionate as he, and, moreover, had not such a profound and confirmed contempt for young women. Yet several times that summer, when driven by lack of amusement to try and engage Lubotshka and Katenka in conversation, I always encountered in them such an absence of any capacity for logical thinking, and such an ignorance of the simplest, most ordinary matters (as, for instance, the nature of money, the subjects studied at universities, the effect of war, and so forth), as well as such indifference to my explanations of such matters, that these attempts of mine only ended in confirming my unfavourable opinion of feminine ability.

I remember one evening when Lubotshka kept repeating some unbearably tedious passage on the piano about a hundred times in succession, while Woloda, who was dozing on a settee in the drawing-room, kept addressing no one in particular as he muttered, "Lord! how she murders it! WHAT a musician! WHAT a Beethoven!" (he always pronounced the composer's name with especial irony). "Wrong again! Now—a second time! That's it!" and so on. Meanwhile Katenka and I were sitting by the tea-table, and somehow she began to talk about her favourite subject—love. I was in the right frame of mind to philosophise, and began by loftily defining love as the wish to acquire in another what one does not possess in oneself. To this Katenka retorted that, on the contrary, love is not love at all if a girl desires to marry a man for his money alone, but that, in her opinion, riches were a vain thing, and true love only the affection which can stand the test of separation (this I took to be a hint concerning her love for Dubkoff). At this point Woloda, who must have been listening all the time, raised himself on his elbow, and cried out some rubbish or another; and I felt that he was right.

Apart from the general faculties (more or less developed in different persons) of intellect, sensibility, and artistic feeling, there also exists (more or less developed in different circles of society, and especially in families) a private or individual faculty which I may call APPREHENSION. The essence of this faculty lies in sympathetic appreciation of proportion, and in identical understanding of things. Two individuals who possess this faculty and belong to the same social circle or the same family apprehend an expression of feeling precisely to the same point, namely, the point beyond which such expression becomes mere phrasing. Thus they apprehend precisely where commendation ends and irony begins, where attraction ends and pretence begins, in a manner which would be impossible for persons possessed of a different order of apprehension. Persons possessed of identical apprehension view objects in an identically ludicrous, beautiful, or repellent light; and in order to facilitate such identical apprehension between members of the same social circle or family, they usually establish a language, turns of speech, or terms to define such shades of apprehension as exist for them alone. In our particular family such apprehension was common to Papa, Woloda, and myself, and was developed to the highest pitch, Dubkoff also approximated to our coterie in apprehension, but Dimitri, though infinitely more intellectual than Dubkoff, was grosser in this respect. With no one, however, did I bring this faculty to such a point as with Woloda, who had grown up with me under identical conditions. Papa stood a long way from us, and much that was to us as clear as "two and two make four" was to him incomprehensible. For instance, I and Woloda managed to establish between ourselves the following terms, with meanings to correspond. Izium (Raisins.) meant a desire to boast of one's money; shishka (Bump or swelling.) (on pronouncing which one had to join one's fingers together, and to put a particular emphasis upon the two sh's in the word) meant anything fresh, healthy, and comely, but not elegant; a substantive used in the plural meant an undue partiality for the object which it denoted; and so forth, and so forth. At the same time, the meaning depended considerably upon the expression of the face and the context of the conversation; so that, no matter what new expression one of us might invent to define a shade of feeling the other could immediately understand it by a hint alone.

The girls did not share this faculty of apprehension, and herein lay the chief cause of our moral estrangement, and of the contempt which we felt for them.

It may be that they too had their "apprehension," but it so little ran with ours that, where we already perceived the "phrasing," they still saw only the feeling—our irony was for them truth, and so on. At that time I had not yet learnt to understand that they were in no way to blame for this, and that absence of such apprehension in no way prevented them from being good and clever girls. Accordingly I looked down upon them. Moreover, having once lit upon my precious idea of "frankness," and being bent upon applying it to the full in myself, I thought the quiet, confiding nature of Lubotshka guilty of secretiveness and dissimulation simply because she saw no necessity for digging up and examining all her thoughts and instincts. For instance, the fact that she always signed the sign of the cross over Papa before going to bed, that she and Katenka invariably wept in church when attending requiem masses for Mamma, and that Katenka sighed and rolled her eyes about when playing the piano—all these things seemed to me sheer make-believe, and I asked myself: "At what period did they learn to pretend like grown-up people, and how can they bring themselves to do it?"

XXX

How I Employed My Time

Nevertheless, the fact that that summer I developed a passion for music caused me to become better friends with the ladies of our household than I had been for years. In the spring, a young fellow came to see us, armed with a letter of introduction, who, as soon as ever he entered the drawing-room, fixed his eyes upon the piano, and kept gradually edging his chair closer to it as he talked to Mimi and Katenka. After discoursing awhile of the weather and the amenities of country life, he skilfully directed the conversation to piano-tuners, music, and pianos generally, and ended by saying that he himself played— and in truth he did sit down and perform three waltzes, with Mimi, Lubotshka, and Katenka grouped about the instrument, and watching him as he did so. He never came to see us again, but his playing, and his attitude when at the piano, and the way in which he kept shaking his long hair, and, most of all, the manner in which he was able to execute octaves with his left hand as he first of all played them rapidly with his thumb and little finger, and then slowly closed those members, and then played the octaves afresh, made a great impression upon me. This graceful gesture of his, together with his easy pose and his shaking of hair and successful winning of the ladies' applause by his talent, ended by firing me to take up the piano. Convinced that I possessed both talent and a passion for music, I set myself to learn, and, in doing so, acted just as millions of the male—still more, of the female—sex have done who try to teach themselves without a skilled instructor, without any real turn for the art, or without the smallest understanding either of what the art can give or of what ought to be done to obtain that gift. For me music (or rather, piano-playing) was simply a means of winning the ladies' good graces through their sensibility. With the help of Katenka I first learnt the notes (incidentally breaking several of them with my clumsy fingers), and then—that is to say, after two months of hard work, supplemented by ceaseless twiddling of my rebellious fingers on my knees after luncheon, and on the pillow when in bed—went on to "pieces," which I played (so Katenka assured me) with "soul" ("avec ame"), but altogether regardless of time.

My range of pieces was the usual one—waltzes, galops, "romances," "arrangements," etcetera; all of them of the class of delightful compositions of which any one with a little healthy taste could point out a selection among the better class works contained in any volume of music and say, "These are what you ought NOT to play, seeing that anything worse, less tasteful, and more silly has never yet been included in any collection of music,"—but which (probably for that very reason) are to be found on the piano of every Russian lady. True, we also possessed an unfortunate volume which contained Beethoven's "Sonate Pathetique" and the C minor Sonata (a volume lamed for life by the ladies—more especially by Lubotshka, who used to discourse music from it in memory of Mamma), as well as certain other good pieces which her teacher in Moscow had given her; but among that collection there were likewise compositions of the teacher's own, in the shape of clumsy marches and galops—and these too Lubotshka used to play! Katenka and I cared nothing for serious works, but preferred, above all things, "Le Fou" and "The Nightingale"—the latter of which Katenka would play until her fingers almost became invisible, and which I too was beginning to execute with much vigour and some continuity. I had adopted the gestures of the young man of whom I have spoken, and frequently regretted that there were no strangers present to see me play. Soon, however, I began to realise that Liszt and Kalkbrenner were beyond me, and that I should never overtake Katenka. Accordingly, imagining that classical music was easier (as well as, partly, for the sake of originality), I suddenly came to the conclusion that I loved abstruse German music. I began to go into raptures whenever Lubotshka played the "Sonate Pathetique," and although (if the truth be told) that work had for years driven me to the verge of distraction, I set myself to play Beethoven, and to talk of him as "Beethoven." Yet through all this chopping and changing and pretence (as I now conceive) there may have run in me a certain vein of talent, since music sometimes affected me even to tears, and things which particularly pleased me I could strum on the piano afterwards (in a certain fashion) without the score; so that, had any one taught me at that period to look upon music as an end, a grace, in itself, and not merely as a means for pleasing womenfolk with the velocity and pseudo-sentiment of one's playing, I might possibly have become a passable musician.

The reading of French novels (of which Woloda had brought a large store with him from Moscow) was another of my amusements that summer. At that period Monte Cristo and Taine's works had just appeared, while I also revelled in stories by Sue, Dumas, and Paul de Kock. Even their most unnatural personages and events were for me as real as actuality, and not only was I incapable of suspecting an author of lying, but, in my eyes, there existed no author at all. That is to say, the various personages and events of a book paraded themselves before me on the printed page as personages and events that were alive and real; and although I had never in my life met such characters as I there read about, I never for a second doubted that I should one day do so. I discovered in myself all the passions described in every novel, as well as a likeness to all the characters—heroes and villains impartially—who figured therein, just as a suspicious man finds in himself the signs of every possible disease when reading a book on medicine. I took pleasure both in the cunning designs, the glowing sentiments, the tumultuous events, and the character-drawing of these works. A good man was of the goodness, a bad man of the badness, possible only to the imagination of early youth. Likewise I found great pleasure in the fact that it was all written in French, and that I could lay to heart the fine words which the fine heroes spoke, and recall them for use some day when engaged in some noble deed. What quantities of French phrases I culled from those books for Kolpikoff's benefit if I should ever meet him again, as well as for HERS, when at length I should find her and reveal to her my love! For them both I prepared speeches which should overcome them as soon as spoken! Upon novels, too, I founded new ideals of the moral qualities which I wished to attain. First of all, I wished to be NOBLE in all my deeds and conduct (I use the French word noble instead of the Russian word blagorodni for the reason that the former has a different meaning to the latter—as the Germans well understood when they adopted noble as nobel and differentiated it from ehrlich); next, to be strenuous; and lastly, to be what I was already inclined to be, namely, comme il faut. I even tried to approximate my appearance and bearing to that of the heroes who possessed these qualities. In particular I remember how in one of the hundred or so novels which I read that summer there was a very strenuous hero with heavy eyebrows, and that I so greatly wished to resemble him (I felt that I did so already from a moral point of view) that one day, when looking at my eyebrows in the glass, I conceived the idea of clipping them, in order to make them grow bushier. Unfortunately, after I had started to do so, I happened to clip one spot rather shorter than the rest, and so had to level down the rest to it-with the result that, to my horror, I beheld myself eyebrow-less, and anything but presentable. However, I comforted myself with the reflection that my eyebrows would soon sprout again as bushy as my hero's, and was only perplexed to think how I could explain the circumstance to the household when they next perceived my eyebrow-less condition. Accordingly I borrowed some gunpowder from Woloda, rubbed it on my temples, and set it alight. The powder did not fire properly, but I succeeded in singeing myself sufficiently to avert all suspicion of my pranks. And, indeed, afterwards, when I had forgotten all about my hero, my eyebrows grew again, and much thicker than they had been before.

XXXI

"Comme Il Faut"

S everal times in the course of this narrative I have hinted at an idea corresponding to the above French heading, and now feel it incumbent upon me to devote a whole chapter to that idea, which was one of the most ruinous, lying notions which ever became engrafted upon my life by my upbringing and social milieu.

The human race may be divided into several categories—rich and poor, good and bad, military and civilian, clever and stupid, and so forth, and so forth. Yet each man has his own favourite, fundamental system of division which he unconsciously uses to class each new person with whom he meets. At the time of which I am speaking, my own favourite, fundamental system of division in this respect was into people "comme il faut" and people "comme il ne faut pas"—the latter subdivided, again, into people merely not "comme il faut" and the lower orders. People "comme il faut" I respected, and looked upon as worthy to consort with me as my equals; the second of the above categories I pretended merely to despise, but in reality hated, and nourished towards them a kind of feeling of offended personality; while the third category had no existence at all, so far as I was concerned, since my contempt for them was too complete. This "comme il faut"-ness of mine lay, first and foremost, in proficiency in French, especially conversational French. A person who spoke that language badly at once aroused in me a feeling of dislike. "Why do you try to talk as we do when you haven't a notion how to do it?" I would seem to ask him with my most venomous and quizzing smile. The second condition of "comme il faut"-ness was long nails that were well kept and clean; the third, ability to bow, dance, and converse; the fourth—and a very important one—indifference to everything, and a constant air of refined, supercilious ennui. Moreover, there were certain general signs which, I considered, enabled me to tell, without actually speaking to a man, the class to which he belonged. Chief among these signs (the others being the fittings of his rooms, his gloves, his handwriting, his turn-out, and so forth) were his feet. The relation of boots to trousers was sufficient to determine, in my eyes, the social status of a man. Heelless boots with angular toes, wedded to narrow, unstrapped trouser-ends—these denoted the vulgarian. Boots with narrow, round toes and heels, accompanied either by tight trousers strapped under the instep and fitting close to the leg or by wide trousers similarly strapped, but projecting in a peak over the toe—these meant the man of mauvais genre; and so on, and so on.

It was a curious thing that I who lacked all ability to become "comme il faut," should have assimilated the idea so completely as I did. Possibly it was the fact that it had cost me such enormous labour to acquire that brought about its strenuous development in my mind. I hardly like to think how much of the best and most valuable time of my first sixteen years of existence I wasted upon its acquisition. Yet every one whom I imitated—Woloda, Dubkoff, and the majority of my acquaintances—seemed to acquire it easily. I watched them with envy, and silently toiled to become proficient in French, to bow gracefully and without looking at the person whom I was saluting, to gain dexterity in small-talk and dancing, to cultivate indifference and ennui, and to keep my fingernails well trimmed (though I frequently cut my finger-ends with the scissors in so doing). And all the time I felt that so much remained to be done if I was ever to attain my end! A room, a writing-table, an equipage I still found it impossible to arrange "comme il faut," however much I fought down my aversion to practical matters in my desire to become proficient. Yet everything seemed to arrange itself properly with other people, just as though things could never have been otherwise! Once I remember asking Dubkoff, after much zealous and careful labouring at my finger-nails (his own were extraordinarily good), whether his nails had always been as now, or whether he had done anything to make them so: to which he replied that never within his recollection had he done anything to them, and that he could not imagine a gentleman's nails possibly being different. This answer incensed me greatly, for I had not yet learnt that one of the chief conditions of "comme il faut"-ness was to hold one's tongue about the labour by which it had been acquired. "Comme il faut"-ness I looked upon as not only a great merit, a splendid accomplishment, an embodiment of all the perfection which must strive to attain, but as the one indispensable condition without which there could never be happiness, nor glory, nor any good whatsoever in this world. Even the greatest artist or savant or benefactor of the human race would at that time have won from me no respect if he had not also been "comme il faut." A man possessed of "comme il faut"-ness stood higher than, and beyond all possible equality with, such people, and might well leave it to them to paint pictures, to compose music, to write books, or to do good. Possibly he might commend them for so doing (since why should not merit be commended where-ever it be found?), but he could never stand ON A LEVEL with them, seeing that he was "comme il faut" and they were not—a quite final and sufficient reason. In fact, I actually believe that, had we possessed a brother or a father or a mother who had not been "comme il faut," I should have declared it to be a great misfortune for us, and announced that between myself and them there could never be anything in common. Yet neither waste of the golden hours which I consumed in constantly endeavouring to observe the many arduous, unattainable conditions of "comme il faut"-ness (to the exclusion of any more serious pursuit), nor dislike of and contempt for nine-tenths of the human race, nor disregard of all the beauty that lay outside the narrow circle of "comme il faut"-ness comprised the whole of the evil which the idea wrought in me. The chief evil of all lay in the notion acquired that a man need not strive to become a tchinovnik, (Official.) a coachbuilder, a soldier, a savant, or anything useful, so long only as he was "comme il faut"—that by attaining the latter quality he had done all that was demanded of him, and was even superior to most people.

Usually, at a given period in youth, and after many errors and excesses, every man recognises the necessity of his taking an active part in social life, and chooses some branch of labour to which to devote himself. Only with the "comme il faut" man does this rarely happen. I have known, and know, very, very many people—old, proud, self-satisfied, and opinionated—who to the question (if it should ever present itself to them in their world) "Who have you been, and what have you ever done?" would be unable to reply otherwise than by saying,

"Je fus un homme tres comme il faut,"

Such a fate was awaiting myself.

XXXII

YOUTH

Despite the confusion of ideas raging in my head, I was at least young, innocent, and free that summer—consequently almost happy.

Sometimes I would rise quite early in the morning, for I slept on the open verandah, and the bright, horizontal beams of the morning sun would wake me up. Dressing myself quickly, I would tuck a towel and a French novel under my arm, and go off to bathe in the river in the shade of a birch tree which stood half a verst from the house. Next, I would stretch myself on the grass and read—raising my eyes from time to time to look at the surface of the river where it showed blue in the shade of the trees, at the ripples caused by the first morning breeze, at the yellowing field of rye on the further bank, and at the bright-red sheen of the sunlight as it struck lower and lower down the white trunks of the birch-trees which, ranged in ranks one behind the other, gradually receded into the remote distance of the home park. At such moments I would feel joyously conscious of having within me the same young, fresh force of life as nature was everywhere exuding around me. When, however, the sky was overcast with grey clouds of morning and I felt chilly after bathing, I would often start to walk at random through the fields and woods, and joyously trail my wet boots in the fresh dew. All the while my head would be filled with vivid dreams concerning the heroes of my last-read novel, and I would keep picturing to myself some leader of an army or some statesman or marvellously strong man or devoted lover or another, and looking round me in, a nervous expectation that I should suddenly descry HER somewhere near me, in a meadow or behind a tree. Yet, whenever these rambles led me near peasants engaged at their work, all my ignoring of the existence of the "common people" did not prevent me from experiencing an involuntary, overpowering sensation of awkwardness; so that I always tried to avoid their seeing me. When the heat of the day had increased, it was not infrequently my habit—if the ladies did not come out of doors for their morning tea—to go rambling through the orchard and kitchen-garden, and to pluck ripe fruit there. Indeed, this was an occupation which furnished me with one of my greatest pleasures. Let any one go into an orchard, and dive into the midst of a tall, thick, sprouting raspberry-bed. Above will be seen the clear, glowing sky, and, all around, the pale-green, prickly stems of raspberry-trees where they grow mingled together in a tangle of profusion. At one's feet springs the dark-green nettle, with its slender crown of flowers, while the broad-leaved burdock, with its bright-pink, prickly blossoms, overtops the raspberries (and even one's head) with its luxuriant masses, until, with the nettle, it almost meets the pendent, pale-green branches of the old apple-trees where apples, round and lustrous as bone, but as yet unripe, are mellowing in the heat of the sun. Below, again, are seen young raspberry-shoots, twining themselves around the partially withered, leafless parent plant, and stretching their tendrils towards the sunlight, with green, needle-shaped blades of grass and young, dew-coated pods peering through last year's leaves, and growing juicily green in the perennial shade, as though they care nothing for the bright sunshine which is playing on the leaves of the apple-trees above them. In this density there is always moisture—always a smell of confined, perpetual shade, of cobwebs, fallen apples (turning black where they roll on the mouldy sod), raspberries, and earwigs of the kind which impel one to reach hastily for more fruit when one has inadvertently swallowed a member of that insect tribe with the last berry. At every step one's movements keep flushing the sparrows which always make their home in these depths, and one hears their fussy chirping and the beating of their tiny, fluttering wings against the stalks, and catches the low buzzing of a bumble bee somewhere, and the sound of the gardener's footsteps (it is half-daft Akim) on the path as he hums his eternal sing-song to himself. Then one mutters under one's breath, "No! Neither he nor any one else shall find me here!" yet still one goes on stripping juicy berries from their conical white pilasters, and cramming them into one's mouth. At length, one's legs soaked to the knees as one repeats, over and over again, some rubbish which keeps running in one's head, and one's hands and nether limbs (despite the protection of one's wet trousers) thoroughly stung with the nettles, one comes to the conclusion that the sun's rays are beating too straight upon one's head for eating to be any longer desirable, and, sinking down into the tangle of greenery, one remains there—

looking and listening, and continuing in mechanical fashion to strip off one or two of the finer berries and swallow them.

At eleven o'clock—that is to say, when the ladies had taken their morning tea and settled down to their occupations—I would repair to the drawing-room. Near the first window, with its unbleached linen blind lowered to exclude the sunshine, but through the chink of which the sun kept throwing brilliant circles of light which hurt the eye to look at them, there would be standing a screen, with flies quietly parading the whiteness of its covering. Behind it would be seated Mimi, shaking her head in an irritable manner, and constantly shifting from spot to spot to avoid the sunshine as at intervals it darted her from somewhere and laid a streak of flame upon her hand or face. Through the other three windows the sun would be throwing three squares of light, crossed with the shadows of the window-frames, and where one of these patches marked the unstained floor of the room there would be lying, in accordance with invariable custom, Milka, with her ears pricked as she watched the flies promenading the lighted space. Seated on a settee, Katenka would be knitting or reading aloud as from time to time she gave her white sleeves (looking almost transparent in the sunshine) an impatient shake, or tossed her head with a frown to drive away some fly which had settled upon her thick auburn hair and was now buzzing in its tangles. Lubotshka would either be walking up and down the room (her hands clasped behind her) until the moment should arrive when a movement would be made towards the garden, or playing some piece of which every note had long been familiar to me. For my own part, I would sit down somewhere, and listen to the music or the reading until such time as I myself should have an opportunity of performing on the piano. After luncheon I would condescend to take the girls out riding (since to go for a mere walk at that hour seemed to me unsuitable to my years and position in the world), and these excursions of ours—in which I often took my companions through unaccustomed spots and dells—were very pleasant. Indeed, on some of these occasions I grew quite boyish, and the girls would praise my riding and daring, and pretend that I was their protector. In the evening, if we had no guests with us, tea (served in the dim verandah), would be followed by a walk round the homestead with Papa, and then I would stretch myself on my usual settee, and read and ponder as of old, as I listened to Katenka or Lubotshka playing. At other times, if I was alone in the drawing-room and Lubotshka was performing some old-time air, I would find myself laying my book down, and gazing through the open doorway on to the balcony at the pendent, sinuous branches of the tall birch-trees where they stood overshadowed by the coming night, and at the clear sky where, if one looked at it intently enough, misty, yellowish spots would appear suddenly, and then disappear again. Next, as I listened to the sounds of the music wafted from the salon, and to the creaking of gates and the voices of the peasant women when the cattle returned to the village, I would suddenly bethink me of Natalia Savishna and of Mamma and of Karl Ivanitch, and become momentarily sad. But in those days my spirit was so full of life and hope that such reminiscences only touched me in passing, and soon fled away again.

After supper and (sometimes) a night stroll with some one in the garden (for I was afraid to walk down the dark avenues by myself), I would repair to my solitary sleeping-place on the verandah—a proceeding which, despite the countless mosquitos which always devoured me, afforded me the greatest pleasure. If the moon was full, I frequently spent whole nights sitting up on my mattress, looking at the light and shade, listening to the sounds or stillness, dreaming of one matter and another (but more particularly of the poetic, voluptuous happiness which, in those days, I believed was to prove the acme of my felicity) and lamenting that until now it had only been given to me to IMAGINE things. No sooner had every one dispersed, and I had seen lights pass from the drawing-room to the upper chambers (whence female voices would presently be heard, and the noise of windows opening and shutting), than I would depart to the verandah, and walk up and down there as I listened attentively to the sounds from the slumbering mansion. To this day, whenever I feel any expectation (no matter how small and baseless) of realising a fraction of some happiness of which I may be dreaming, I somehow invariably fail to picture to myself what the imagined happiness is going to be like.

At the least sound of bare footsteps, or of a cough, or of a snore, or of the rattling of a window, or of the rustling of a dress, I would leap from my mattress, and stand furtively gazing and listening, thrown, without any visible cause, into extreme agitation. But the lights would disappear from the upper rooms, the sounds of footsteps and talking give place to snores, the watchman begin his nightly tapping with his stick, the garden grow brighter and more mysterious as the streaks of light vanished from the windows, the last candle pass from the pantry to the hall (throwing a glimmer into the dewy garden as it did so), and the stooping figure of Foka (decked in a nightcap, and carrying the candle) become visible to my eyes as he went to his bed. Often I would find a great and fearful pleasure in stealing over the grass, in the black shadow of the house, until I had reached the hall window, where I would stand listening with bated breath to the snoring of the boy, to Foka's gruntings (in the belief that no one heard him), and to the sound of his senile voice as he drawled out the evening prayers. At length even his candle would be extinguished, and the window slammed down, so that I would find myself utterly alone; whereupon, glancing nervously from side to side, lest haply I should see the white woman standing near a flower-bed or by my couch, I would run at full speed back to the verandah. Then, and only then, I would lie down with my face to the garden, and, covering myself over, so far as possible, from the mosquitos and bats, fall to gazing in front of me as I listened to the sounds of the night and dreamed of love and happiness.

At such times everything would take on for me a different meaning. The look of the old birch trees, with the one side of their curling branches showing bright against the moonlit sky, and the other darkening the bushes and carriage-drive with their black shadows; the calm, rich glitter of the pond, ever swelling like a sound; the moonlit sparkle of the dewdrops on the flowers in front of the verandah; the graceful shadows of those flowers where they lay thrown upon the grey stonework; the cry of a quail on the far side of the pond; the voice of some one walking on the high road; the quiet, scarcely audible scrunching of two old birch trees against one another; the humming of a mosquito at my car under the coverlet; the fall of an apple as it caught against a branch and rustled among the dry leaves; the leapings of frogs as they approached almost to the verandah-steps and sat with the moon shining mysteriously on their green backs—all these things took on for me a strange significance—a significance of exceeding beauty and of infinite love. Before me would rise SHE, with long black tresses and a high bust, but always mournful in her fairness, with bare hands and voluptuous arms. She loved me, and for one moment of her love I would sacrifice my whole life!—But the moon would go on rising higher and higher, and shining brighter and brighter, in the heavens; the rich sparkle of the pond would swell like a sound, and become ever more and more brilliant, while the shadows would grow blacker and blacker, and the sheen of the moon more and more transparent: until, as I looked at and listened to all this, something would say to me that SHE with the bare hands and voluptuous arms did not represent ALL happiness, that love for her did not represent ALL good; so that, the more I gazed at the full, high-riding moon, the higher would true beauty and goodness appear to me to lie, and the purer and purer they would seem—the nearer and nearer to Him who is the source of all beauty and all goodness. And tears of a sort of unsatisfied, yet tumultuous, joy would fill my eyes.

Always, too, I was alone; yet always, too, it seemed to me that, although great, mysterious Nature could draw the shining disc of the moon to herself, and somehow hold in some high, indefinite place the pale-blue sky, and be everywhere around me, and fill of herself the infinity of space, while I was but a lowly worm, already defiled with the poor, petty passions of humanity—always it seemed to me that, nevertheless, both Nature and the moon and I were one.

XXXIII

Our Neighbours

On the first day after our arrival, I had been greatly astonished that Papa should speak of our neighbours, the Epifanovs, as "nice people," and still more so that he should go to call upon them. The fact was that we had long been at law over some land with this family. When a child, I had more than once heard Papa raging over the litigation, abusing the Epifanovs, and warning people (so I understood him) against them. Likewise, I had heard Jakoff speak of them as "our enemies" and "black people" and could remember Mamma requesting that their names should never be mentioned in her presence, nor, indeed, in the house at all.

From these data I, as a child, had arrived at the clear and assured conviction that the Epifanovs were foemen of ours who would at any time stab or strangle both Papa and his sons if they should ever come across them, as well as that they were "black people", in the literal sense of the term. Consequently, when, in the year that Mamma died, I chanced to catch sight of Avdotia ("La Belle Flamande") on the occasion of a visit which she paid to my mother, I found it hard to believe that she did not come of a family of negroes. All the same, I had the lowest possible opinion of the family, and, for all that we saw much of them that summer, continued to be strongly prejudiced against them. As a matter of fact, their household only consisted of the mother (a widow of fifty, but a very well-preserved, cheery old woman), a beautiful daughter named Avdotia, and a son, Peter, who was a stammerer, unmarried, and of very serious disposition.

For the last twenty years before her husband's death, Madame Epifanov had lived apart from him—sometimes in St. Petersburg, where she had relatives, but more frequently at her village of Mitishtchi, which stood some three versts from ours. Yet the neighbourhood had taken to circulating such horrible tales concerning her mode of life that Messalina was, by comparison, a blameless child: which was why my mother had requested her name never to be mentioned. As a matter of fact, not one-tenth part of the most cruel of all gossip—the gossip of country-houses—is worthy of credence; and although, when

I first made Madame's acquaintance, she had living with her in the house a clerk named Mitusha, who had been promoted from a serf, and who, curled, pomaded, and dressed in a frockcoat of Circassian pattern, always stood behind his mistress's chair at luncheon, while from time to time she invited her guests to admire his handsome eyes and mouth, there was nothing for gossip to take hold of. I believe, too, that since the time—ten years earlier—when she had recalled her dutiful son Peter from the service, she had wholly changed her mode of living. It seems her property had never been a large one—merely a hundred souls or so—(This refers, of course, to the days of serfdom.) and that during her previous life of gaiety she had spent a great deal. Consequently, when, some ten years ago, those portions of the property which had been mortgaged and re-mortgaged had been foreclosed upon and compulsorily sold by auction, she had come to the conclusion that all these unpleasant details of distress upon and valuation of her property had been due not so much to failure to pay the interest as to the fact that she was a woman: wherefore she had written to her son (then serving with his regiment) to come and save his mother from her embarrassments, and he, like a dutiful son—conceiving that his first duty was to comfort his mother in her old age—had straightway resigned his commission (for all that he had been doing well in his profession, and was hoping soon to become independent), and had come to join her in the country.

Despite his plain face, uncouth demeanour, and fault of stuttering, Peter was a man of unswerving principles and of the most extraordinary good sense. Somehow—by small borrowings, sundry strokes of business, petitions for grace, and promises to repay—he contrived to carry on the property, and, making himself overseer, donned his father's greatcoat (still preserved in a drawer), dispensed with horses and carriages, discouraged guests from calling at Mitishtchi, fashioned his own sleighs, increased his arable land and curtailed that of the serfs, felled his own timber, sold his produce in person, and saw to matters generally. Indeed, he swore, and kept his oath, that, until all outstanding debts were paid, he would never wear any clothes than his father's greatcoat and a corduroy jacket which he had made for himself, nor yet ride in aught but a country waggon, drawn by peasants' horses. This stoical mode of life he sought to apply also to his family, so far as the sympathetic respect which he conceived to be his mother's due would allow of; so that, although, in the drawing-room, he would show her only stuttering servility, and fulfil all her wishes, and blame any one who did not do precisely as she bid them, in his study or his office he would overhaul the cook if she had served up so much as a duck without his orders, or any one responsible for sending a serf (even though at Madame's own bidding) to inquire after a neighbour's health or for despatching the peasant girls into the wood to gather wild raspberries instead of setting them to weed the kitchen-garden.

Within four years every debt had been repaid, and Peter had gone to Moscow and returned thence in a new jacket and tarantass. (A two-wheeled carriage.) Yet, despite this flourishing position of affairs, he still preserved the stoical tendencies in which, to tell the truth, he took a certain vague pride before his family and strangers, since he would frequently say with a stutter: "Any one who REALLY wishes to see me will be glad to see me even in my dressing-gown, and to eat nothing but shtchi (Cabbage-soup.) and kasha (Buckwheat gruel.) at my table." "That is what I eat myself," he would add. In his every word and movement spoke pride based upon a consciousness of having sacrificed himself for his mother and redeemed the property, as well as contempt for any one who had not done something of the same kind.

The mother and daughter were altogether different characters from Peter, as well as altogether different from one another. The former was one of the most agreeable, uniformly good-tempered, and cheerful women whom one could possibly meet. Anything attractive and genuinely happy delighted her. Even the faculty of being pleased with the sight of young people enjoying themselves (it is only in the best-natured of elderly folk that one meets with that TRAIT) she possessed to the full. On the other hand, her daughter was of a grave turn of mind. Rather, she was of that peculiarly careless, absent-minded, gratuitously distant bearing which commonly distinguishes unmarried beauties. Whenever she tried to be gay, her gaiety somehow seemed to be unnatural to her, so that she always appeared to be laughing either at herself or at the persons to whom she was speaking or at the world in general—a thing which, possibly, she had no real intention of doing. Often I asked myself in astonishment what she could mean when she said something like, "Yes, I know how terribly good-looking I am," or, "Of course every one is in love with me," and so forth. Her mother was a person always busy, since she had a passion for housekeeping, gardening, flowers, canaries, and pretty trinkets. Her rooms and garden, it is true, were small and poorly fitted-up, yet everything in them was so neat and methodical, and bore such a general air of that gentle gaiety which one hears expressed in a waltz or polka, that the word "toy" by which guests often expressed their praise of it all exactly suited her surroundings. She herself was a "toy"—being petite, slender, fresh-coloured, small, and pretty-handed, and invariably gay and well-dressed. The only fault in her was that a slight over-prominence of the dark-blue veins on her little hands rather marred the general effect of her appearance. On the other hand, her daughter scarcely ever did anything at all. Not only had she no love for trifling with flowers and trinkets, but she neglected her personal exterior, and only troubled to dress herself well when guests happened to call. Yet, on returning to the room in society costume, she always looked extremely handsome—save for that cold, uniform expression of eyes and smile which is common to all beauties. In fact, her strictly regular, beautiful face and symmetrical figure always seemed to be saying to you, "Yes, you may look at me."

At the same time, for all the mother's liveliness of disposition and the daughter's air of indifference and abstraction, something told one that the former was incapable of feeling affection for anything that was not pretty and gay, but that Avdotia, on the contrary, was one of those natures which, once they love, are willing to sacrifice their whole life for the man they adore.

XXXIV

My Father's Second Marriage

My father was forty-eight when he took as his second wife Avdotia Vassilievna Epifanov.

I suspect that when, that spring, he had departed for the country with the girls, he had been in that communicatively happy, sociable mood in which gamblers usually find themselves who have retired from play after winning large stakes. He had felt that he still had a fortune left to him which, so long as he did not squander it on gaming, might be used for our advancement in life. Moreover, it was springtime, he was unexpectedly well supplied with ready money, he was alone, and he had nothing to do. As he conversed with Jakoff on various matters, and remembered both the interminable suit with the Epifanovs and Avdotia's beauty (it was a long while since he had seen her), I can imagine him saying: "How do you think we ought to act in this suit, Jakoff? My idea is simply to let the cursed land go. Eh? What do you think about it?" I can imagine, too, how, thus interrogated, Jakoff twirled his fingers behind his back in a deprecatory sort of way, and proceeded to argue that it all the same, "Peter Alexandritch, we are in the right." Nevertheless, I further conjecture, Papa ordered the dogcart to be got ready, put on his fashionable olive-coloured driving-coat, brushed up the remnants of his hair, sprinkled his clothes with scent, and, greatly pleased to think that he was acting a la seignior (as well as, even more, revelling in the prospect of soon seeing a pretty woman), drove off to visit his neighbours.

I can imagine, too, that when the flustered housemaid ran to inform Peter Vassilievitch that Monsieur Irtenieff himself had called, Peter answered angrily, "Well, what has he come for?" and, stepping softly about the house, first went into his study to put on his old soiled jacket, and then sent down word to the cook that on no account whatever—no, not even if she were ordered to do so by the mistress herself—was she to add anything to luncheon.

Since, later, I often saw Papa with Peter, I can form a very good idea of this first interview between them. I can imagine that, despite Papa's proposal to end the suit in a peaceful manner, Peter was morose and resentful at the thought of having sacrificed his career to his mother, and at Papa having done nothing of the kind—a by no means surprising circumstance, Peter probably said to himself. Next, I can see Papa taking no notice of this ill-humour, but cracking quips and jests, while Peter gradually found himself forced to treat him as a humorist with whom he felt offended one moment and inclined to be reconciled the next. Indeed, with his instinct for making fun of everything, Papa often used to address Peter as "Colonel;" and though I can remember Peter once replying, with an unusually violent stutter and his face scarlet with indignation, that he had never been a c-c-colonel, but only a l-l-lieutenant, Papa called him "Colonel" again before another five minutes were out.

Lubotshka told me that, up to the time of Woloda's and my arrival from Moscow, there had been daily meetings with the Epifanovs, and that things had been very lively, since Papa, who had a genius for arranging, everything with a touch of originality and wit, as well as in a simple and refined manner, had devised shooting and fishing parties and fireworks for the Epifanovs' benefit. All these festivities—so said Lubotshka—would have gone off splendidly but for the intolerable Peter, who had spoilt everything by his puffing and stuttering. After our coming, however, the Epifanovs only visited us twice, and we went once to their house, while after St. Peter's Day (on which, it being Papa's nameday, the Epifanovs called upon us in common with a crowd of other guests) our relations with that family came entirely to an end, and, in future, only Papa went to see them.

During the brief period when I had opportunities of seeing Papa and Dunetchka (as her mother called Avdotia) together, this is what I remarked about them. Papa remained unceasingly in the same buoyant mood as had so greatly struck me on the day after our arrival. So gay and youthful and full of life and happy did he seem that the beams of his felicity extended themselves to all around him, and involuntarily communicated to them a similar frame of mind. He never stirred from Avdotia's side so long as she was in the room, but either kept on plying her with sugary-sweet compliments which made me feel ashamed for him or, with his gaze fixed upon her with an air at once passionate and complacent, sat hitching his shoulder and coughing as from time to time he smiled and whispered something in her ear. Yet throughout he wore the same expression of raillery as was peculiar to him even in the most serious matters.

As a rule, Avdotia herself seemed to catch the infection of the happiness which sparkled at this period in Papa's large blue eyes; yet there were moments also when she would be seized with such a fit of shyness that I, who knew the feeling well, was full of sympathy and compassion as I regarded her embarrassment. At moments of this kind she seemed to be afraid of every glance and every movement—to be supposing that every one was looking at her, every one thinking of no one but her, and that unfavourably. She would glance timidly from one person to another, the colour coming and going in her cheeks, and then begin to talk loudly and defiantly, but, for the most part, nonsense; until presently, realising this, and supposing that Papa and every one else had heard her, she would blush more painfully than ever. Yet Papa never noticed her nonsense, for he was too much taken up with coughing and with gazing at her with his look of happy, triumphant devotion. I noticed, too, that, although these fits of shyness attacked Avdotia, without any visible cause, they not infrequently ensued upon Papa's mention of one or another young and beautiful woman. Frequent transitions from depression to that strange, awkward gaiety of hers to which I have referred before the repetition of favourite words and turns of speech of Papa's; the continuation of discussions with others which Papa had already begun—all these things, if my father had not been the principal actor in the matter and I had been a little older, would have explained to me the relations subsisting between him and Avdotia. At the time, however, I never surmised them—no, not even when Papa received from her brother Peter a letter which so upset him that not again until the end of August did he go to call upon the Epifanovs'. Then, however, he began his visits once more, and ended by informing us, on the day before Woloda and I were to return to Moscow, that he was about to take Avdotia Vassilievna Epifanov to be his wife.

XXXV

How We Received the News

Yet, even on the eve of the official announcement, every one had learnt of the matter, and was discussing it. Mimi never left her room that day, and wept copiously. Katenka kept her company, and only came out for luncheon, with a grieved expression on her face which was manifestly borrowed from her mother. Lubotshka, on the contrary, was very cheerful, and told us after luncheon that she knew of a splendid secret which she was going to tell no one.

"There is nothing so splendid about your secret," said Woloda, who did not in the least share her satisfaction. "If you were capable of any serious thought at all, you would understand that it is a very bad lookout for us."

Lubotshka stared at him in amazement, and said no more. After the meal was over, Woloda made a feint of taking me by the arm, and then, fearing that this would seem too much like "affection," nudged me gently by the elbow, and beckoned me towards the salon.

"You know, I suppose, what the secret is of which Lubotshka was speaking?" he said when he was sure that we were alone. It was seldom that he and I spoke together in confidence: with the result that, whenever it came about, we felt a kind of awkwardness in one another's presence, and "boys began to jump about" in our eyes, as Woloda expressed it. On the present occasion, however, he answered the excitement in my eyes with a grave, fixed look which said: "You need not be surprised, for we are brothers, and we have to consider an important family matter." I understood him, and he went on:

"You know, I suppose, that Papa is going to marry Avdotia Epifanov?"

I nodded, for I had already heard so. "Well, it is not a good thing," continued Woloda.

"Why so?"

"Why?" he repeated irritably. "Because it will be so pleasant, won't it, to have this stuttering 'colonel' and all his family for relations! Certainly she seems nice enough, as yet; but who knows what she will turn out to be later? It won't matter much to you or myself, but Lubotshka will soon be making her debut, and it will hardly be nice for her to have such a 'belle mere' as this—a woman who speaks French badly, and has no manners to teach her."

Although it seemed odd to hear Woloda criticising Papa's choice so coolly, I felt that he was right.

"Why is he marrying her?" I asked.

"Oh, it is a hole-and-corner business, and God only knows why," he answered. "All I know is that her brother, Peter, tried to make conditions about the marriage, and that, although at first Papa would not hear of them, he afterwards took some fancy or knight-errantry or another into his head. But, as I say, it is a hole-and-corner business. I am only just beginning to understand my father"—the fact that Woloda called Papa "my father" instead of "Papa" somehow hurt me—"and though I can see that he is kind and clever, he is irresponsible and frivolous to a degree that—Well, the whole thing is astonishing. He cannot so much as look upon a woman calmly. You yourself know how he falls in love with every one that he meets. You know it, and so does Mimi."

"What do you mean?" I said.

"What I say. Not long ago I learnt that he used to be in love with Mimi herself when he was a young man, and that he used to send her poetry, and that there really was something between them. Mimi is heart-sore about it to this day"—and Woloda burst out laughing.

"Impossible!" I cried in astonishment.

"But the principal thing at this moment," went on Woloda, becoming serious again, and relapsing into French, "is to think how delighted all our relations will be with this marriage! Why, she will probably have children!"

Woloda's prudence and forethought struck me so forcibly that I had no answer to make. Just at this moment Lubotshka approached us.

"So you know?" she said with a joyful face.

"Yes," said Woloda. "Still, I am surprised at you, Lubotshka. You are no longer a baby in long clothes. Why should you be so pleased because Papa is going to marry a piece of trash?"

At this Lubotshka's face fell, and she became serious.

"Oh, Woloda!" she exclaimed. "Why 'a piece of trash' indeed? How can you dare to speak of Avdotia like that? If Papa is going to marry her she cannot be 'trash.'"

"No, not trash, so to speak, but—"

"No 'buts' at all!" interrupted Lubotshka, flaring up. "You have never heard me call the girl whom you are in love with 'trash!' How, then, can you speak so of Papa and a respectable woman? Although you are my elder brother, I won't allow you to speak like that! You ought not to!"

"Mayn't I even express an opinion about—"

"No, you mayn't!" repeated Lubotshka. "No one ought to criticise such a father as ours. Mimi has the right to, but not you, however much you may be the eldest brother."

"Oh you don't understand anything," said Woloda contemptuously. "Try and do so. How can it be a good thing that a 'Dunetchka' of an Epifanov should take the place of our dead Mamma?"

For a moment Lubotshka was silent. Then the tears suddenly came into her eyes.

"I knew that you were conceited, but I never thought that you could be cruel," she said, and left us.

"Pshaw!" said Woloda, pulling a serio-comic face and make-believe, stupid eyes. "That's what comes of arguing with them." Evidently he felt that he was at fault in having so far forgot himself as to descend to discuss matters at all with Lubotshka.

Next day the weather was bad, and neither Papa nor the ladies had come down to morning tea when I entered the drawing-room. There had been cold rain in the night, and remnants of the clouds from which it had descended were still scudding across the sky, with the sun's luminous disc (not yet risen to any great height) showing faintly through them. It was a windy, damp, grey morning. The door into the garden was standing open, and pools left by the night's rain were drying on the damp-blackened flags of the terrace. The open door was swinging on its iron hinges in the wind, and all the paths looked wet and muddy. The old birch trees with their naked white branches, the bushes, the turf, the nettles, the currant-trees, the elders with the pale side of their leaves turned upwards—all were dashing themselves about, and looking as though they were trying to wrench themselves free from their roots. From the avenue of lime-trees showers of round, yellow leaves were flying through the air in tossing, eddying circles, and strewing the wet road and soaked aftermath of the hayfield with a clammy carpet. At the moment, my thoughts were wholly taken up with my father's approaching marriage and with the point of view from which Woloda regarded it. The future seemed to me to bode no good for any of us. I felt distressed to think that a woman who was not only a stranger but young should be going to associate with us in so many relations of life, without having any right to do so—nay, that this young woman was going to usurp the place of our dead mother. I felt depressed, and kept thinking more and more that my father was to blame in the matter. Presently I heard his voice and Woloda's speaking together in the pantry, and, not wishing to meet Papa just then, had just left the room when I was pursued by Lubotshka, who said that Papa wanted to see me.

He was standing in the drawing-room, with his hand resting on the piano, and was gazing in my direction with an air at once grave and impatient. His face no longer wore the youthful, gay expression which had struck me for so long, but, on the contrary, looked sad. Woloda was walking about the room with a pipe in his hand. I approached my father, and bade him good morning.

"Well, my children," he said firmly, with a lift of his head and in the peculiarly hurried manner of one who wishes to announce something obviously unwelcome, but no longer admitting of reconsideration, "you know, I suppose, that I am going to marry Avdotia Epifanov." He paused a moment. "Hitherto I had had no desire for any one to succeed your mother, but"—and again he paused—"it-it is evidently my fate. Dunetchka is an excellent, kind girl, and no longer in her first youth. I hope, therefore, my children, that you will like her, and she, I know, will be sincerely fond of you, for she is a good woman. And now," he went on, addressing himself more particularly to Woloda and myself, and having the appearance of speaking hurriedly in order to prevent us from interrupting him, "it is time for you to depart, while I myself am going to stay here until the New Year, and then to follow you to Moscow with"—again he hesitated a moment—"my wife and Lubotshka." It hurt me to see my father standing as though abashed and at fault before us, so I moved a little nearer him, but Woloda only went on walking about the room with his head down, and smoking.

"So, my children, that is what your old father has planned to do," concluded Papa—reddening, coughing, and offering Woloda and myself his hands. Tears were in his eyes as he said this, and I noticed, too, that the hand which he was holding out to Woloda (who at that moment chanced to be at the other end of the room) was shaking slightly. The sight of that shaking hand gave me an unpleasant shock, for I remembered that Papa had served in 1812, and had been, as every one knew, a brave officer. Seizing the great veiny hand, I covered it with kisses, and he squeezed mine hard in return. Then, with a sob amid his tears, he suddenly threw his arms around Lubotshka's dark head, and kissed her again and again on the eyes. Woloda pretended that he had dropped his pipe, and, bending down, wiped his eyes furtively with the back of his hand. Then, endeavouring to escape notice, he left the room.

XXXVI

THE UNIVERSITY

The wedding was to take place in two weeks' time, but, as our lectures had begun already, Woloda and myself were forced to return to Moscow at the beginning of September. The Nechludoffs had also returned from the country, and Dimitri (with whom, on parting, I had made an agreement that we should correspond frequently with the result, of course, that we had never once written to one another) came to see us immediately after our arrival, and arranged to escort me to my first lecture on the morrow.

It was a beautiful sunny day. No sooner had I entered the auditorium than I felt my personality entirely disappear amid the swarm of light-hearted youths who were seething tumultuously through every doorway and corridor under the influence of the sunlight pouring through the great windows. I found the sense of being a member of this huge community very pleasing, yet there were few among the throng whom I knew, and that only on terms of a nod and a "How do you do, Irtenieff?"

All around me men were shaking hands and chatting together—from every side came expressions of friendship, laughter, jests, and badinage. Everywhere I could feel the tie which bound this youthful society in one, and everywhere, too, I could feel that it left me out. Yet this impression lasted for a moment only, and was succeeded, together with the vexation which it had caused, by the idea that it was best that I should not belong to that society, but keep to my own circle of gentlemen; wherefore I proceeded to seat myself upon the third bench, with, as neighbours, Count B., Baron Z., the Prince R., Iwin, and some other young men of the same class with none of whom, however, was acquainted save with Iwin and Count B. Yet the look which these young gentlemen threw at me at once made me feel that I was not of their set, and I turned to observe what was going on around me. Semenoff, with grey, matted hair, white teeth, and tunic flying open, was seated a little distance off, and leaning forward on his elbows as he nibbled a pen, while the gymnasium student who had come out first in the examinations had established himself on the front bench, and, with a black stock coming half-way up his cheek, was toying with the silver watch-chain which adorned his satin waistcoat. On a bench in a raised part of the hall I could descry Ikonin (evidently he had contrived to enter the University somehow!), and hear him fussily proclaiming, in all the glory of blue piped trousers which completely hid his boots, that he was now seated on Parnassus. Ilinka—who had surprised me by giving me a bow not only cold, but supercilious, as though to remind me that here we were all equals—was just in front of me, with his legs resting in free and easy style on another bench (a hit, somehow I thought, at myself), and conversing with a student as he threw occasional glances in my direction. Iwin's set by my side were talking in French, yet every word which I overheard of their conversation seemed to me both stupid and incorrect ("Ce n'est pas francais," I thought to myself), while all the attitudes, utterances, and doings of Semenoff, Ilinka, and the rest struck me as uniformly coarse, ungentlemanly, and "comme il ne faut pas."

Thus, attached to no particular set, I felt isolated and unable to make friends, and so grew resentful. One of the students on the bench in front of me kept biting his nails, which were raw to the quick already, and this so disgusted me that I edged away from him. In short, I remember finding my first day a most depressing affair.

When the professor entered, and there was a general stir and a cessation of chatter, I remember throwing a scornful glance at him, as also that he began his discourse with a sentence which I thought devoid of meaning. I had expected the lecture to be, from first to last, so clever that not a word ought to be taken from or added to it. Disappointed in this, I at once proceeded to draw beneath the heading "First Lecture" with which I had adorned my beautifully-bound notebook no less than eighteen faces in profile, joined together in a sort of chaplet, and only occasionally moved my hand along the page in order to give the professor (who, I felt sure, must be greatly interested in me) the impression that I was writing something. In fact, at this very first lecture I came to the decision which I maintained to the end of my course, namely, that it was unnecessary, and even stupid, to take down every word said by every professor.

At subsequent lectures, however, I did not feel my isolation so strongly, since I made several acquaintances and got into the way of shaking hands and entering into conversation. Yet for some reason or another no real intimacy ever sprang up between us, and I often found myself depressed and only feigning cheerfulness. With the set which comprised Iwin and "the aristocrats," as they were generally known, I could not make any headway at all, for, as I now remember, I was always shy and churlish to them, and nodded to them only when they nodded to me; so that they had little inducement to desire my acquaintance. With most of the other students, however, this arose from quite a different cause. As soon as ever I discerned friendliness on the part of a comrade, I at once gave him to understand that I went to luncheon with Prince Ivan Ivanovitch and kept my own drozhki. All this I said merely to show myself in the most favourable light in his eyes, and to induce him to like me all the more; yet almost invariably the only result of my communicating to him the intelligence concerning the drozhki and my relationship to Prince Ivan Ivanovitch was that, to my astonishment, he at once adopted a cold and haughty bearing towards me.

Among us we had a Crown student named Operoff—a very modest, industrious, and clever young fellow, who always offered one his hand like a slab of wood (that is to say, without closing his fingers or making the slightest movement with them); with the result that his comrades often did the same to him in jest, and called it the "deal board" way of shaking hands. He and I nearly always sat next to one another, and discussed matters generally. In particular he pleased me with the freedom with which he would criticise the professors as he pointed out to me with great clearness and acumen the merits or demerits of their respective ways of teaching and made occasional fun of them. Such remarks I found exceedingly striking and diverting when uttered in his quiet, mincing voice. Nevertheless he never let a lecture pass without taking careful notes of it in his fine handwriting, and eventually we decided to join forces, and to do our preparation together. Things had progressed to the point of his always looking pleased when I took my usual seat beside him when, unfortunately, I one day found it necessary to inform him that, before her death, my mother had besought my father never to allow us to enter for a government scholarship, as well as that I myself considered Crown students, no matter how clever, to be "well, they are not GENTLEMEN," I concluded, though beginning to flounder a little and grow red. At the moment Operoff said nothing, but at subsequent lectures he ceased to greet me or to offer me his board-like hand, and never attempted to talk to me, but, as soon as ever I sat down, he would lean his head upon his arm, and purport to be absorbed in his notebooks. I was surprised at this sudden coolness, but looked upon it as infra dig, "pour un jeune homme de bonne maison" to curry favour with a mere Crown student of an Operoff, and so left him severely alone—though I confess that his aloofness hurt my feelings. On one occasion I arrived before him, and, since the lecture was to be delivered by a popular professor whom students came to hear who did not usually attend such functions, I found almost every seat occupied. Accordingly I secured Operoff's place for myself by spreading my notebooks on the desk before it; after which I left the room again for a moment. When I returned I perceived that my paraphernalia had been relegated to the bench behind, and the place taken by Operoff himself. I remarked to him that I had already secured it by placing my notebooks there.

"I know nothing about that," he replied sharply, yet without looking up at me.

"I tell you I placed my notebooks there," I repeated, purposely trying to bluster, in the hope of intimidating him. "Every one saw me do it," I added, including the students near me in my glance. Several of them looked at me with curiosity, yet none of them spoke.

"Seats cannot be booked here," said Operoff. "Whoever first sits down in a place keeps it," and, settling himself angrily where he was, he flashed at me a glance of defiance.

"Well, that only means that you are a cad," I said.

I have an idea that he murmured something about my being "a stupid young idiot," but I decided not to hear it. What would be the use, I asked myself, of my hearing it? That we should brawl like a couple of manants over less than nothing? (I was very fond of the word manants, and often used it for meeting awkward junctures.) Perhaps I should have said something more had not, at that moment, a door slammed and the professor (dressed in a blue frockcoat, and shuffling his feet as he walked) ascended the rostrum.

Nevertheless, when the examination was about to come on, and I had need of some one's notebooks, Operoff remembered his promise to lend me his, and we did our preparation together.

XXXVII

Affaires of the Heart

Affaires du coeur exercised me greatly that winter. In fact, I fell in love three times. The first time, I became passionately enamoured of a buxom lady whom I used to see riding at Freitag's riding-school; with the result that every day when she was taking a lesson there (that is to say, every Tuesday and Friday) I used to go to gaze at her, but always in such a state of trepidation lest I should be seen that I stood a long way off, and bolted directly I thought her likely to approach the spot where I was standing. Likewise, I used to turn round so precipitately whenever she appeared to be glancing in my direction that I never saw her face well, and to this day do not know whether she was really beautiful or not.

Dubkoff, who was acquainted with her, surprised me one day in the riding-school, where I was lurking concealed behind the lady's grooms and the fur wraps which they were holding, and, having heard from Dimitri of my infatuation, frightened me so terribly by proposing to introduce me to the Amazon that I fled incontinently from the school, and was prevented by the mere thought that possibly he had told her about me from ever entering the place again, or even from hiding behind her grooms, lest I should encounter her.

Whenever I fell in love with ladies whom I did not know, and especially married women, I experienced a shyness a thousand times greater than I had ever felt with Sonetchka. I dreaded beyond measure that my divinity should learn of my passion, or even of my existence, since I felt sure that, once she had done so, she would be so terribly offended that I should never be forgiven for my presumption. And indeed, if the Amazon referred to above had ever come to know how I used to stand behind the grooms and dream of seizing her and carrying her off to some country spot—if she had ever come to know how I should have lived with her there, and how I should have treated her, it is probable that she would have had very good cause for indignation! But I always felt that, once I got to know her, she would straightway divine these thoughts, and consider herself insulted by my acquaintance.

As my second affaire du coeur, I, (for the third time) fell in love with Sonetchka when I saw her at her sister's. My second passion for her had long since come to an end, but I became enamoured of her this third time through Lubotshka sending me a copy-book in which Sonetchka had copied some extracts from Lermontoff's The Demon, with certain of the more subtly amorous passages underlined in red ink and marked with pressed flowers. Remembering how Woloda had been wont to kiss his inamorata's purse last year, I essayed to do the same thing now; and really, when alone in my room in the evenings and engaged in dreaming as I looked at a flower or occasionally pressed it to my lips, I would feel a certain pleasantly lachrymose mood steal over me, and remain genuinely in love (or suppose myself to be so) for at least several days.

Finally, my third affaire du coeur that winter was connected with the lady with whom Woloda was in love, and who used occasionally to visit at our house. Yet, in this damsel, as I now remember, there was not a single beautiful feature to be found—or, at all events, none of those which usually pleased me. She was the daughter of a well-known Moscow lady of light and leading, and, petite and slender, wore long flaxen curls after the English fashion, and could boast of a transparent profile. Every one said that she was even cleverer and more learned than her mother, but I was never in a position to judge of that, since, overcome with craven bashfulness at the mere thought of her intellect and accomplishments, I never spoke to her alone but once, and then with unaccountable trepidation. Woloda's enthusiasm, however (for the presence of an audience never prevented him from giving vent to his rapture), communicated itself to me so strongly that I also became enamoured of the lady. Yet, conscious that he would not be pleased to know that two brothers were in love with the same girl, I never told him of my condition. On the contrary, I took special delight in the thought that our mutual love for her was so pure that, though its object was, in both cases, the same charming being, we remained friends and ready, if ever the occasion should arise, to sacrifice ourselves for one another. Yet I have an idea that, as regards self-sacrifice, he did not quite share my views, for he was so passionately in love with the lady that once he was for giving a member of the diplomatic corps, who was said to be going to marry her, a slap in the face and a challenge to a duel; but, for my part, I would gladly have sacrificed my feelings for his sake, seeing that the fact that the only remark I had ever addressed to her had been on the subject of the dignity of classical music, and that my passion, for all my efforts to keep it alive, expired the following week, would have rendered it the more easy for me to do so.

XXXVIII

The World

As regards those worldly delights to which I had intended, on entering the University, to surrender myself in imitation of my brother, I underwent a complete disillusionment that winter. Woloda danced a great deal, and Papa also went to balls with his young wife, but I appeared to be thought either too young or unfitted for such delights, and no one invited me to the houses where balls were being given. Yet, in spite of my vow of frankness with Dimitri, I never told him (nor any one else) how much I should have liked to go to those dances, and how I felt hurt at being forgotten and (apparently) taken for the philosopher that I pretended to be.

Nevertheless, a reception was to be given that winter at the Princess Kornakoff's, and to it she sent us personal invitations—to myself among the rest! Consequently, I was to attend my first ball. Before starting, Woloda came into my room to see how I was dressing myself—an act on his part which greatly surprised me and took me aback. In my opinion (it must be understood) solicitude about one's dress was a shameful thing, and should be kept under, but he seemed to think it a thing so natural and necessary that he said outright that he was afraid I should be put out of countenance on that score. Accordingly, he bid me don my patent leather boots, and was horrified to find that I wanted to put on gloves of peau de chamois. Next, he adjusted my watch-chain in a particular manner, and carried me off to a hairdresser's near the Kuznetski Bridge to have my locks coiffured. That done, he withdrew to a little distance and surveyed me.

"Yes, he looks right enough now" said he to the hairdresser. "Only—couldn't you smooth those tufts of his in front a little?" Yet, for all that Monsieur Charles treated my forelocks with one essence and another, they persisted in rising up again when ever I put on my hat. In fact, my curled and tonsured figure seemed to me to look far worse than it had done before. My only hope of salvation lay in an affectation of untidiness. Only in that guise would my exterior resemble anything at all. Woloda, apparently, was of the same opinion, for he begged me to undo the curls, and when I had done so and still looked unpresentable, he ceased to regard me at all, but throughout the drive to the Kornakoffs remained silent and depressed.

Nevertheless, I entered the Kornakoffs' mansion boldly enough, and it was only when the Princess had invited me to dance, and I, for some reason or another (though I had driven there with no other thought in my head than to dance well), had replied that I never indulged in that pastime, that I began to blush, and, left solitary among a crowd of strangers, became plunged in my usual insuperable and ever-growing shyness. In fact, I remained silent on that spot almost the whole evening!

Nevertheless, while a waltz was in progress, one of the young princesses came to me and asked me, with the sort of official kindness common to all her family, why I was not dancing. I can remember blushing hotly at the question, but at the same time feeling—for all my efforts to prevent it—a self-satisfied smile steal over my face as I began talking, in the most inflated and long-winded French, such rubbish as even now, after dozens of years, it shames me to recall. It must have been the effect of the music, which, while exciting my nervous sensibility, drowned (as I supposed) the less intelligible portion of my utterances. Anyhow, I went on speaking of the exalted company present, and of the futility of men and women, until I had got myself into such a tangle that I was forced to stop short in the middle of a word of a sentence which I found myself powerless to conclude.

Even the worldly-minded young Princess was shocked by my conduct, and gazed at me in reproach; whereat I burst out laughing. At this critical moment, Woloda, who had remarked that I was conversing with great animation, and probably was curious to know what excuses I was making for not dancing, approached us with Dubkoff. Seeing, however, my smiling face and the Princess's frightened mien, as well as overhearing the appalling rubbish with which I concluded my speech, he turned red in the face, and wheeled round again. The Princess also rose and left me. I continued to smile, but in such a state of agony from the consciousness of my stupidity that I felt ready to sink into the floor. Likewise I felt that, come what might, I must move about and say something, in order to effect a change in my position. Accordingly I approached Dubkoff, and asked him if he had danced many waltzes with her that night. This I feigned to say in a gay and jesting manner, yet in reality I was imploring help of the very Dubkoff to whom I had cried "Hold your tongue!" on the night of the matriculation dinner. By way of answer, he made as though he had not heard me, and turned away. Next, I approached Woloda, and said with an effort and in a similar tone of assumed gaiety: "Hullo, Woloda! Are you played out yet?" He merely looked at me as much as to say, "You wouldn't speak to me like that if we were alone," and left me without a word, in the evident fear that I might continue to attach myself to his person.

"My God! Even my own brother deserts me!" I thought to myself.

Yet somehow I had not the courage to depart, but remained standing where I was until the very end of the evening. At length, when every one was leaving the room and crowding into the hall, and a footman slipped my greatcoat on to my shoulders in such a way as to tilt up my cap, I gave a dreary, half-lachrymose smile, and remarked to no one in particular: "Comme c'est gracieux!"

XXXIX

The Students' Feast

Notwithstanding that, as yet, Dimitri's influence had kept me from indulging in those customary students' festivities known as kutezhi or "wines," that winter saw me participate in such a function, and carry away with me a not over-pleasant impression of it. This is how it came about.

At a lecture soon after the New Year, Baron Z.—a tall, light-haired young fellow of very serious demeanour and regular features—invited us all to spend a sociable evening with him. By "us all", I mean all the men more or less "comme il faut", of our course, and exclusive of Grap, Semenoff, Operoff, and commoners of that sort. Woloda smiled contemptuously when he heard that I was going to a "wine" of first course men, but I looked to derive great and unusual pleasure from this, to me, novel method of passing the time. Accordingly, punctually at the appointed hour of eight I presented myself at the Baron's.

Our host, in an open tunic and white waistcoat, received his guests in the brilliantly lighted salon and drawing-room of the small mansion where his parents lived—they having given up their reception rooms to him for the evening for purposes of this party. In the corridor could be seen the heads and skirts of inquisitive domestics, while in the dining-room I caught a glimpse of a dress which I imagined to belong to the Baroness herself. The guests numbered a score, and were all of them students except Herr Frost (in attendance upon Iwin) and a tall, red-faced gentleman who was superintending the feast and who was introduced to every one as a relative of the Baron's and a former student of the University of Dorpat. At first, the excessive brilliancy and formal appointments of the reception-rooms had such a chilling effect upon this youthful company that every one involuntarily hugged the walls, except a few bolder spirits and the ex-Dorpat student, who, with his waistcoat already unbuttoned, seemed to be in every room, and in every corner of every room, at once, and filled the whole place with his resonant, agreeable, never-ceasing tenor voice. The remainder of the guests preferred either to remain silent or to talk in discreet tones of professors, faculties, examinations, and other serious and interesting matters. Yet every one, without exception, kept watching the door of the dining-room, and, while trying to conceal the fact, wearing an expression which said: "Come! It is time to begin." I too felt that it was time to begin, and awaited the beginning with pleasurable impatience.

After footmen had handed round tea among the guests, the Dorpat student asked Frost in Russian:

"Can you make punch, Frost?"

"Oh ja!" replied Frost with a joyful flourish of his heels, and the other went on:

"Then do you set about it" (they addressed each other in the second person singular, as former comrades at Dorpat). Frost accordingly departed to the dining-room, with great strides of his bowed, muscular legs, and, after some walking backwards and forwards, deposited upon the drawing-room table a large punchbowl, accompanied by a ten-pound sugar loaf supported on three students' swords placed crosswise. Meanwhile, the Baron had been going round among his guests as they sat regarding the punch-bowl, and addressing them, with a face of immutable gravity, in the formula: "I beg of you all to drink of this loving-cup in student fashion, that there may be good-fellowship among the members of our course. Unbutton your waistcoats, or take them off altogether, as you please." Already the Dorpat student had divested himself of his tunic and rolled up his white shirt-sleeves above his elbows, and now, planting his feet firmly apart, he proceeded to set fire to the rum in the punch-bowl.

"Gentlemen, put out the candles!" he cried with a sudden shout so loud and insistent that we seemed all of us to be shouting at once. However, we still went on silently regarding the punch-bowl and the white shirt of the Dorpat student, with a feeling that a moment of great solemnity was approaching.

"Put out the lights, Frost, I tell you!" the Dorpat student shouted again. Evidently the punch was now sufficiently burnt. Accordingly every one helped to extinguish the candles, until the room was in total darkness save for a spot where the white shirts and hands of the three students supporting the sugarloaf on their crossed swords were lit up by the lurid flames from the bowl. Yet the Dorpat student's tenor voice was not the only one to be heard, for in different quarters of the room resounded chattering and laughter. Many had taken off their tunics (especially students whose garments were of fine cloth and perfectly new), and I now did the same, with a consciousness that "It" was "beginning." There had been no great festivity as yet, but I felt assured that things would go splendidly when once we had begun drinking tumblers of the potion that was now in course of preparation.

At length, the punch was ready, and the Dorpat student, with much bespattering of the table as he did so, ladled the liquor into tumblers, and cried: "Now, gentlemen, please!" When we had each of us taken a sticky tumbler of the stuff into our hands, the Dorpat student and Frost sang a German song in which the word "Hoch!" kept occurring again and again, while we joined, in haphazard fashion, in the chorus. Next we clinked glasses together, shouted something in praise of punch, crossed hands, and took our first drink of the sweet, strong mixture. After that there was no further waiting; the "wine" was in full swing. The first glassful consumed, a second was poured out. Yet, for all that I began to feel a throbbing in my temples, and that the flames seemed to be turning purple, and that every one around me was laughing and shouting, things seemed lacking in real gaiety, and I somehow felt that, as a matter of fact, we were all of us finding the affair rather dull, and only PRETENDING to be enjoying it. The Dorpat student may have been an exception, for he continued to grow more and more red in the face and more and more ubiquitous as he filled up empty glasses and stained the table with fresh spots of the sweet, sticky stuff. The precise sequence of events I cannot remember, but I can recall feeling strongly attracted towards Frost and the Dorpat student that evening, learning their German song by heart, and kissing them each on their sticky-sweet lips; also that that same evening I conceived a violent hatred against the Dorpat student, and was for pushing him from his chair, but thought better of it; also that, besides feeling the same spirit of independence towards the rest of the company as I had felt on the night of the matriculation dinner, my head ached and swam so badly that I thought each moment would be my last; also that, for some reason or another, we all of us sat down on the floor and imitated the movements of rowers in a boat as we sang in chorus, "Down our mother stream the Volga;" also that I conceived this procedure on our part to be uncalled for; also that, as I lay prone upon the floor, I crossed my legs and began wriggling about like a tsigane; (Gipsy dancer.) also that I ricked some one's neck, and came to the conclusion that I should never have done such a thing if I had not been drunk; also that we had some supper and another kind of liquor, and that I then went to the door to get some fresh air; also that my head seemed suddenly to grow chill, and that I noticed, as I drove away, that the scat of the vehicle was so sharply aslant and slippery that for me to retain my position behind Kuzma was impossible; also that he seemed to have turned all flabby, and to be waving about like a dish clout. But what I remember best is that throughout the whole of that evening I never ceased to feel that I was acting with excessive stupidity in pretending to be enjoying myself, to like drinking a great deal, and to be in no way drunk, as well as that every one else present was acting with equal stupidity in pretending those same things. All the time I had a feeling that each one of my companions was finding the festivities as distasteful as I was myself; but, in the belief that he was the only one doing so, felt himself bound to pretend that he was very merry, in order not to mar the general hilarity. Also, strange to state, I felt that I ought to keep up this pretence for the sole reason that into a punch-bowl there had been poured three bottles of champagne at nine roubles the bottle and ten bottles of rum at four—making seventy roubles in all, exclusive of the supper. So convinced of my folly did I feel that, when, at next day's lecture, those of my comrades who had been at Baron Z.'s party seemed not only in no way ashamed to remember what they had done, but even talked about it so that other students might hear of their doings, I felt greatly astonished. They all declared that it had been a splendid "wine," that Dorpat students were just the fellows for that kind of thing, and that there had been consumed at it no less than forty bottles of rum among twenty guests, some of whom had dropped senseless under the table! That they should care to talk about such things seemed strange enough, but that they should care to lie about them seemed absolutely unintelligible.

XL

My Friendship with the Nechludoffs

That winter, too, I saw a great deal both of Dimitri who often looked us up, and of his family, with whom I was beginning to stand on intimate terms.

The Nechludoffs (that is to say, mother, aunt, and daughter) always spent their evenings at home, at which time the Princess liked young men to visit her—at all events young men of the kind whom she described as able to spend an evening without playing cards or dancing. Yet such young fellows must have been few and far between, for, although I went to the Nechludoffs almost every evening, I seldom found other guests present. Thus, I came to know the members of this family and their several dispositions well enough to be able to form clear ideas as to their mutual relations, and to be quite at home amid the rooms and furniture of their house. Indeed, so long as no other guests were present, I felt entirely at my ease. True, at first I used to feel a little uncomfortable when left alone in the room with Varenika, for I could not rid myself of the idea that, though far from pretty, she wished me to fall in love with her; but in time this nervousness of mine began to lessen, since she always looked so natural, and talked to me so exactly as though she were conversing with her brother or Lubov Sergievna, that I came to look upon her simply as a person to whom it was in no way dangerous or wrong to show that I took pleasure in her company. Throughout the whole of our acquaintance she appeared to me merely a plain, though not positively ugly, girl, concerning whom one would never ask oneself the question,

"Am I, or am I not, in love with her?" Sometimes I would talk to her direct, but more often I did so through Dimitri or Lubov Sergievna; and it was the latter method which afforded me the most pleasure. I derived considerable gratification from discoursing when she was there, from hearing her sing, and, in general, from knowing that she was in the same room as myself; but it was seldom now that any thoughts of what our future relations might ever be, or that any dreams of self-sacrifice for my friend if he should ever fall in love with my sister, came into my head. If any such ideas or fancies occurred to me, I felt satisfied with the present, and drove away all thoughts about the future.

Yet, in spite of this intimacy, I continued to look upon it as my bounden duty to keep the Nechludoffs in general, and Varenika in particular, in ignorance of my true feelings and tastes, and strove always to appear altogether another young man than what I really was—to appear, indeed, such a young man as could never possibly have existed. I affected to be "soulful" and would go off into raptures and exclamations and impassioned gestures whenever I wished it to be thought that anything pleased me, while, on the other hand, I tried always to seem indifferent towards any unusual circumstance which I myself perceived or which I had had pointed out to me. I aimed always at figuring both as a sarcastic cynic divorced from every sacred tie and as a shrewd observer, as well as at being accounted logical in all my conduct, precise and methodical in all my ways of life, and at the same time contemptuous of all materiality. I may safely say that I was far better in reality than the strange being into whom I attempted to convert myself; yet, whatever I was or was not, the Nechludoffs were unfailingly kind to me, and (happily for myself) took no notice (as it now appears) of my play-acting. Only Lubov Sergievna, who, I believe, really believed me to be a great egoist, atheist, and cynic, had no love for me, but frequently disputed what I said, flew into tempers, and left me petrified with her disjointed, irrelevant utterances. Yet Dimitri held always to the same strange, something more than friendly, relations with her, and used to say not only that she was misunderstood by every one, but that she did him a world of good. This, however, did not prevent the rest of his family from finding fault with his infatuation.

Once, when talking to me about this incomprehensible attachment, Varenika explained the matter thus: "You see, Dimitri is a selfish person. He is very proud, and, for all his intellect, very fond of praise, and of surprising people, and of always being First, while little Auntie" (the general nickname for Lubov Sergievna) "is innocent enough to admire him, and at the same time devoid of the tact to conceal her admiration. Consequently she flatters his vanity—not out of pretence, but sincerely."

This dictum I laid to heart, and, when thinking it over afterwards, could not but come to the conclusion that Varenika was very sensible; wherefore I was glad to award her promotion thenceforth in my regard. Yet, though I was always glad enough to assign her any credit which might arise from my discovering in her character any signs of good sense or other moral qualities, I did so with strict moderation, and never ran to any extreme pitch of enthusiasm in the process. Thus, when

Sophia Ivanovna (who was never weary of discussing her niece) related to me how, four years ago, Varenika had suddenly given away all her clothes to some peasant children without first asking permission to do so, so that the garments had subsequently to be recovered, I did not at once accept the fact as entitling Varenika to elevation in my opinion, but went on giving her good advice about the unpracticalness of such views on property.

When other guests were present at the Nechludoffs (among them, sometimes, Woloda and Dubkoff) I used to withdraw myself to a remote plane, and, with the complacency and quiet consciousness of strength of an habitue of the house, listen to what others were saying without putting in a remark myself. Yet everything that these others said seemed to me so immeasurably stupid that I used to feel inwardly amazed that such a clever, logical woman as the Princess, with her equally logical family, could listen to and answer such rubbish. Had it, however, entered into my head to compare what, others said with what I myself said when there alone, I should probably have ceased to feel surprise. Still less should I have continued to feel surprise had I not believed that the women of our own household—Avdotia, Lubotshka, and Katenka—were superior to the rest of their sex, for in that case I should have remembered the kind of things over which Avdotia and Katenka would laugh and jest with Dubkoff from one end of an evening to the other. I should have remembered that seldom did an evening pass but Dubkoff would first have, an argument about something, and then read in a sententious voice either some verses beginning "Au banquet de la vie, infortune convive" or extracts from The Demon. In short, I should have remembered what nonsense they used to chatter for hours at a time.

It need hardly be said that, when guests were present, Varenika paid less attention to me than when we were alone, as well as that I was deprived of the reading and music which I so greatly loved to hear. When talking to guests, she lost, in my eyes, her principal charm—that of quiet seriousness and simplicity. I remember how strange it used to seem to me to hear her discoursing on theatres and the weather to my brother Woloda! I knew that of all things in the world he most despised and shunned banality, and that Varenika herself used to make fun of forced conversations on the weather and similar matters. Why, then, when meeting in society, did they both of them talk such intolerable nothings, and, as it were, shame one another? After talks of this kind I used to feel silently resentful against Woloda, as well as next day to rally Varenika on her overnight guests. Yet one result of it was that I derived all the greater pleasure from being one of the Nechludoffs' family circle. Also, for some reason or another I began to prefer meeting Dimitri in his mother's drawing-room to being with him alone.

XLI

My Friendship with the Nechludoffs (continued)

At this period, indeed, my friendship with Dimitri hung by a hair. I had been criticising him too long not to have discovered faults in his character, for it is only in first youth that we love passionately and therefore love only perfect people. As soon as the mists engendered by love of this kind begin to dissolve, and to be penetrated by the clear beams of reason, we see the object of our adoration in his true shape, and with all his virtues and failings exposed. Some of those failings strike us with the exaggerated force of the unexpected, and combine with the instinct for novelty and the hope that perfection may yet be found in a fellow-man to induce us not only to feel coldness, but even aversion, towards the late object of our adoration. Consequently, desiring it no longer, we usually cast it from us, and pass onwards to seek fresh perfection. For the circumstance that that was not what occurred with respect to my own relation to Dimitri, I was indebted to his stubborn, punctilious, and more critical than impulsive attachment to myself—a tie which I felt ashamed to break. Moreover, our strange vow of frankness bound us together. We were afraid that, if we parted, we should leave in one another's power all the incriminatory moral secrets of which we had made mutual confession. At the same time, our rule of frankness had long ceased to be faithfully observed, but, on the contrary, proved a frequent cause of constraint, and brought about strange relations between us.

Almost every time that winter that I went upstairs to Dimitri's room, I used to find there a University friend of his named Bezobiedoff, with whom he appeared to be very much taken up. Bezobiedoff was a small, slight fellow, with a face pitted over with smallpox, freckled, effeminate hands, and a huge flaxen moustache much in need of the comb. He was invariably dirty, shabby, uncouth, and uninteresting. To me, Dimitri's relations with him were as unintelligible as his relations with Lubov Sergievna, and the only reason he could have had for choosing such a man for his associate was that in the whole University there was no worse-looking student than Bezobiedoff. Yet that alone would have been sufficient to make Dimitri extend him his friendship, and, as a matter of fact, in all his intercourse with this fellow he seemed to be saying proudly: "I care nothing who a man may be. In my eyes every one is equal. I like him, and therefore he is a desirable acquaintance." Nevertheless I could not imagine how he could bring himself to do it, nor how the wretched Bezobiedoff ever contrived to maintain his awkward position. To me the friendship seemed a most distasteful one.

One night, I went up to Dimitri's room to try and get him to come down for an evening's talk in his mother's drawing-room, where we could also listen to Varenika's reading and singing, but Bezobiedoff had forestalled me there, and Dimitri answered me curtly that he could not come down, since, as I could see for myself, he had a visitor with him.

"Besides," he added, "what is the fun of sitting there? We had much better stay HERE and talk."

I scarcely relished the prospect of spending a couple of hours in Bezobiedoff's company, yet could not make up my mind to go down alone; wherefore, cursing my friend's vagaries, I seated myself in a rocking-chair, and began rocking myself silently to and fro. I felt vexed with them both for depriving me of the pleasures of the drawing-room, and my only hope as I listened irritably to their conversation was that Bezobiedoff would soon take his departure. "A nice guest indeed to be sitting with!" I thought to myself when a footman brought in tea and Dimitri had five times to beg Bezobiedoff to have a cup, for the reason that the bashful guest thought it incumbent upon him always to refuse it at first and to say, "No, help yourself." I could see that Dimitri had to put some restraint upon himself as he resumed the conversation. He tried to inveigle me also into it, but I remained glum and silent.

"I do not mean to let my face give any one the suspicion that I am bored" was my mental remark to Dimitri as I sat quietly rocking myself to and fro with measured beat. Yet, as the moments passed, I found myself—not without a certain satisfaction—growing more and more inwardly hostile to my friend. "What a fool he is!" I reflected. "He might be spending the evening agreeably with his charming family, yet he goes on sitting with this brute!—will go on doing so, too, until it is too late to go down to the drawing-room!" Here I glanced at him over the back of my chair, and thought the general look of his attitude and appearance so offensive and repellant that at the moment I could gladly have offered him some insult, even a most serious one.

At last Bezobiedoff rose, but Dimitri could not easily let such a delightful friend depart, and asked him to stay the night. Fortunately,

Bezobiedoff declined the invitation, and departed. Having seen him off, Dimitri returned, and, smiling a faintly complacent smile as he did so, and rubbing his hands together (in all probability partly because he had sustained his character for eccentricity, and partly because he had got rid of a bore), started to pace the room, with an occasional glance at myself. I felt more offended with him than ever. "How can he go on walking about the room and grinning like that?" was my inward reflection.

"What are you so angry about?" he asked me suddenly as he halted in front of my chair.

"I am not in the least angry," I replied (as people always do answer under such circumstances). "I am merely vexed that you should play-act to me, and to Bezobiedoff, and to yourself."

"What rubbish!" he retorted. "I never play-act to any one."

"I have in mind our rule of frankness," I replied, "when I tell you that I am certain you cannot bear this Bezobiedoff any more than I can. He is an absolute cad, yet for some inexplicable reason or another it pleases you to masquerade before him."

"Not at all! To begin with, he is a splendid fellow, and—"

"But I tell you it Is so. I also tell you that your friendship for Lubov Sergievna is founded on the same basis, namely, that she thinks you a god."

"And I tell you once more that it is not so."

"Oh, I know it for myself," I retorted with the heat of suppressed anger, and designing to disarm him with my frankness. "I have told you before, and I repeat it now, that you always seem to like people who say pleasant things to you, but that, as soon as ever I come to examine your friendship, I invariably find that there exists no real attachment between you."

"Oh, but you are wrong," said Dimitri with an angry straightening of the neck in his collar. "When I like people, neither their praise nor their blame can make any difference to my opinion of them."

"Well, dreadful though it may seem to you, I confess that I myself often used to hate my father when he abused me, and to wish that he was dead. In the same way, you—"

"Speak for yourself. I am very sorry that you could ever have been so—"

"No, no!" I cried as I leapt from my chair and faced him with the courage of exasperation. "It is for Yourself that you ought to feel sorry—sorry because you never told me a word about this fellow. You know that was not honourable of you. Nevertheless, I will tell You what I think of you," and, burning to wound him even more than he had wounded me, I set out to prove to him that he was incapable of feeling any real affection for anybody, and that I had the best of grounds (as in very truth I believed I had) for reproaching him. I took great pleasure in telling him all this, but at the same time forgot that the only conceivable purpose of my doing so—to force him to confess to the faults of which I had accused him—could not possibly be attained at the present moment, when he was in a rage. Had he, on the other hand, been in a condition to argue calmly, I should probably never have said what I did.

The dispute was verging upon an open quarrel when Dimitri suddenly became silent, and left the room. I pursued him, and continued what I was saying, but he did not answer. I knew that his failings included a hasty temper, and that he was now fighting it down; wherefore I cursed his good resolutions the more in my heart.

This, then, was what our rule of frankness had brought us to—the rule that we should "tell one another everything in our minds, and never discuss one another with a third person!" Many a time we had exaggerated frankness to the pitch of making mutual confession of the most shameless thoughts, and of shaming ourselves by voicing to one another proposals or schemes for attaining our desires; yet those confessions had not only failed to draw closer the tie which united us, but had dissipated sympathy and thrust us further apart, until now pride would not allow him to expose his feelings even in the smallest detail, and we employed in our quarrel the very weapons which we had formerly surrendered to one another—the weapons which could strike the shrewdest blows!

LEO TOLSTOY

XLII

OUR STEPMOTHER

Notwithstanding that Papa had not meant to return to Moscow before the New Year, he arrived in October, when there was still good riding to hounds to be had in the country. He alleged as his reason for changing his mind that his suit was shortly to come on before the Senate, but Mimi averred that Avdotia had found herself so ennuyee in the country, and had so often talked about Moscow and pretended to be unwell, that Papa had decided to accede to her wishes. "You see, she never really loved him—she and her love only kept buzzing about his ears because she wanted to marry a rich man," added Mimi with a pensive sigh which said: "To think what a certain other person could have done for him if only he had valued her!"

Yet that "certain other person" was unjust to Avdotia, seeing that the latter's affection for Papa—the passionate, devoted love of self-abandonment—revealed itself in her every look and word and movement. At the same time, that love in no way hindered her, not only from being averse to parting with her adored husband, but also from desiring to visit Madame Annette's and order there a lovely cap, a hat trimmed with a magnificent blue ostrich feather, and a blue Venetian velvet bodice which was to expose to the public gaze the snowy, well shaped breast and arms which no one had yet gazed upon except her husband and maids. Of course Katenka sided with her mother and, in general, there became established between Avdotia and ourselves, from the day of her arrival, the most extraordinary and burlesque order of relations. As soon as she stepped from the carriage, Woloda assumed an air of great seriousness and ceremony, and, advancing towards her with much bowing and scraping, said in the tone of one who is presenting something for acceptance:

"I have the honour to greet the arrival of our dear Mamma, and to kiss her hand."

"Ah, my dear son!" she replied with her beautiful, unvarying smile.

"And do not forget the younger son," I said as I also approached her hand, with an involuntary imitation of Woloda's voice and expression.

Had our stepmother and ourselves been certain of any mutual affection, that expression might have signified contempt for any outward manifestation of our love. Had we been ill-disposed towards one another, it might have denoted irony, or contempt for pretence, or a desire to conceal from Papa (standing by the while) our real relations, as well as many other thoughts and sentiments. But, as a matter of fact, that expression (which well consorted with Avdotia's own spirit) simply signified nothing at all—simply concealed the absence of any definite relations between us. In later life I often had occasion to remark, in the case of other families whose members anticipated among themselves relations not altogether harmonious, the sort of provisional, burlesque relations which they formed for daily use; and it was just such relations as those which now became established between ourselves and our stepmother. We scarcely ever strayed beyond them, but were polite to her, conversed with her in French, bowed and scraped before her, and called her "chere Maman"—a term to which she always responded in a tone of similar lightness and with her beautiful, unchanging smile. Only the lachrymose Lubotshka, with her goose feet and artless prattle, really liked our stepmother, or tried, in her naive and frequently awkward way, to bring her and ourselves together: wherefore the only person in the world for whom, besides Papa, Avdotia had a spark of affection was Lubotshka. Indeed, Avdotia always treated her with a kind of grave admiration and timid deference which greatly surprised me.

From the first Avdotia was very fond of calling herself our stepmother and hinting that, since children and servants usually adopt an unjust and hostile attitude towards a woman thus situated, her own position was likely to prove a difficult one. Yet, though she foresaw all the unpleasantness of her predicament, she did nothing to escape from it by (for instance) conciliating this one, giving presents to that other one, and forbearing to grumble—the last a precaution which it would have been easy for her to take, seeing that by nature she was in no way exacting, as well as very good-tempered. Yet, not only did she do none of these things, but her expectation of difficulties led her to adopt the defensive before she had been attacked. That is to say, supposing that the entire household was designing to show her every kind of insult and annoyance, she would see plots where no plots were, and consider that her most dignified course was to suffer in silence—an attitude of passivity as regards winning AFfection which of course led to DISaffection. Moreover, she was so totally lacking in that faculty of "apprehension" to which I have already referred as being highly developed in our household, and all her customs were so utterly opposed to those which had long been rooted in our establishment, that those two facts alone were bound to go against her. From the first, her mode of life in our tidy, methodical household was that of a person only just arrived there. Sometimes she went to bed late, sometimes early; sometimes she appeared at luncheon, sometimes she did not; sometimes she took supper, sometimes she dispensed with it. When we had no guests with us she more often than not walked about the house in a semi-nude condition, and was not ashamed to appear before us—even before the servants—in a white chemise, with only a shawl thrown over her bare shoulders. At first this Bohemianism pleased me, but before very long it led to my losing the last shred of respect which I felt for her. What struck me as even more strange was the fact that, according as we had or had not guests, she was two different women. The one (the woman figuring in society) was a young and healthy, but rather cold, beauty, a person richly dressed, neither stupid nor clever, and unfailingly cheerful. The other woman (the one in evidence when no guests were present) was considerably past her first youth, languid, depressed, slovenly, and ennuyee, though affectionate. Frequently, as I looked at her when, smiling, rosy with the winter air, and happy in the consciousness of her beauty, she came in from a round of calls and, taking off her hat, went to look at herself in a mirror; or when, rustling in her rich, decollete ball dress, and at once shy and proud before the servants, she was passing to her carriage; or when, at one of our small receptions at home, she was sitting dressed in a high silken dress finished with some sort of fine lace about her soft neck, and flashing her unvarying, but lovely, smile around her—as I looked at her at such times I could not help wondering what would have been said by persons who had been ravished to behold her thus if they could have seen her as I often saw her, namely, when, waiting in the lonely midnight hours for her husband to return from his club, she would walk like a shadow from room to room, with her hair dishevelled and her form clad in a sort of dressing-jacket. Presently, she would sit down to the piano and, her brows all puckered with the effort, play over the only waltz that she knew; after which she would pick up a novel, read a few pages somewhere in the middle of it, and throw it aside. Next, repairing in person to the dining-room, so as not to disturb the servants, she would get herself a cucumber and some cold veal, and eat it standing by the window-sill—then once more resume her weary, aimless, gloomy wandering from room to room. But what, above all other things, caused estrangement between us was that lack of understanding which expressed itself chiefly in the peculiar air of indulgent attention with which she would listen when any one was speaking to her concerning matters of which she had no knowledge. It was not her fault that she acquired the unconscious habit of bending her head down and smiling slightly with her lips only when she found it necessary to converse on topics which did not interest her (which meant any topic except herself and her husband); yet that smile and that inclination of the head, when incessantly repeated, could become unbearably wearisome. Also, her peculiar gaiety—which always sounded as though she were laughing at herself, at you, and at the world in general—was gauche and anything but infectious, while her sympathy was too evidently forced. Lastly, she knew no reticence with regard to her ceaseless rapturising to all and sundry concerning her love for Papa. Although she only spoke the truth when she said that her whole life was bound up with him, and although she proved it her life long, we considered such unrestrained, continual insistence upon her affection for him bad form, and felt more ashamed for her when she was descanting thus before strangers even than we did when she was perpetrating bad blunders in French. Yet, although, as I have said, she loved her husband more than anything else in the world, and he too had a great affection for her (or at all events he had at first, and when he saw that others besides himself admired her beauty), it seemed almost as though she purposely did everything most likely to displease him—simply to prove to him the strength of her love, her readiness to sacrifice herself for his sake, and the fact that her one aim in life was to win his affection! She was fond of display, and my father too liked to see her as a beauty who excited wonder and admiration; yet she sacrificed her weakness for fine clothes to her love for him, and grew more and more accustomed to remain at home in a plain grey blouse. Again, Papa considered freedom and equality to be indispensable conditions of family life, and hoped that his favourite Lubotshka and his kind-hearted young wife would become sincere friends; yet once again Avdotia sacrificed herself by considering it incumbent upon her to pay the "real mistress of the house," as she called Lubotshka, an amount of deference which only shocked and annoyed my father. Likewise, he played cards a great deal that winter, and lost considerable sums towards the end of it, wherefore, unwilling, as usual, to let his gambling affairs intrude upon his family life, he began to preserve complete secrecy concerning his play; yet Avdotia, though often ailing, as well as, towards the end of the winter, enceinte, considered herself bound always to sit up (in a grey blouse, and with her hair dishevelled) for my father when, at, say, four or five o'clock in the morning, he returned home from the club ashamed, depleted in pocket, and weary. She would ask him absent-mindedly whether he had been fortunate in play, and listen with indulgent attention, little nods of her head, and a faint smile upon her face as he told her of his doings at the club and begged her, for about the hundredth time, never to sit up for him again. Yet, though Papa's winnings or losings (upon which his substance practically depended) in no way interested her, she was always the first to meet him when he returned home in the small hours of the morning. This she was incited to do, not only by the strength of her devotion, but by a certain secret jealousy from which she suffered. No one in the world could persuade her that it was REALLY from his club, and not from a mistress's, that Papa came home so late. She would try to read love secrets in his face, and, discerning none there, would sigh with a sort of enjoyment of her grief, and give herself up once more to the contemplation of her unhappiness.

As the result of these and many other constant sacrifices which occurred in Papa's relations with his wife during the latter months of that winter (a time when he lost much, and was therefore out of spirits), there gradually grew up between the two an intermittent feeling of tacit hostility—of restrained aversion to the object of devotion of the kind which expresses itself in an unconscious eagerness to show the object in question every possible species of petty annoyance.

XLIII

New Comrades

The winter had passed imperceptibly and the thaw begun when the list of examinations was posted at the University, and I suddenly remembered that I had to return answers to questions in eighteen subjects on which I had heard lectures delivered, but with regard to some of which I had taken no notes and made no preparation whatever. It seems strange that the question "How am I going to pass?" should never have entered my head, but the truth is that all that winter I had been in such a state of haze through the delights of being both grown-up and "comme il faut" that, whenever the question of the examinations had occurred to me, I had mentally compared myself with my comrades, and thought to myself, "They are certain to pass, and as most of them are not 'comme il faut,' and I am therefore their personal superior, I too am bound to come out all right." In fact, the only reason why I attended lectures at all was that I might become an habitue of the University, and obtain Papa's leave to go in and out of the house. Moreover, I had many acquaintances now, and often enjoyed myself vastly at the University. I loved the racket, talking, and laughter in the auditorium, the opportunities for sitting on a back bench, and letting the measured voice of the professor lure one into dreams as one contemplated one's comrades, the occasional runnings across the way for a snack and a glass of vodka (sweetened by the fearful joy of knowing that one might be hauled before the professor for so doing), the stealthy closing of the door as one returned to the auditorium, and the participation in "course versus course" scuffles in the corridors. All this was very enjoyable.

By the time, however, that every one had begun to put in a better attendance at lectures, and the professor of physics had completed his course and taken his leave of us until the examinations came on, and the students were busy collecting their notebooks and arranging to do their preparation in parties, it struck me that I also had better prepare for the ordeal. Operoff, with whom I still continued on bowing, but otherwise most frigid, terms, suddenly offered not only to lend me his notebooks, but to let me do my preparation with himself and some other students. I thanked him, and accepted the invitation—hoping by that conferment of honour completely to dissipate our old misunderstanding; but at the same time I requested that the gatherings should always be held at my home, since my quarters were so splendid! To this the students replied that they meant to take turn and turn about—sometimes to meet at one fellow's place, sometimes at another's, as might be most convenient.

The first of our reunions was held at Zuchin's, who had a small partition-room in a large building on the Trubni Boulevard. The opening night I arrived late, and entered when the reading aloud had already begun. The little apartment was thick with tobacco-smoke, while on the table stood a bottle of vodka, a decanter, some bread, some salt, and a shin-bone of mutton. Without rising, Zuchin asked me to have some vodka and to doff my tunic.

"I expect you are not accustomed to such entertainment," he added.

Every one was wearing a dirty cotton shirt and a dickey. Endeavouring not to show my contempt for the company, I took off my tunic, and lay down in a sociable manner on the sofa. Zuchin went on reading aloud and correcting himself with the help of notebooks, while the others occasionally stopped him to ask a question, which he always answered with ability, correctness, and precision. I listened for a time with the rest, but, not understanding much of it, since I had not been present at what had been read before, soon interpolated a question.

"Hullo, old fellow! It will be no good for you to listen if you do not know the subject," said Zuchin. "I will lend you my notebooks, and then you can read it up by tomorrow, and I will explain it to you."

I felt rather ashamed of my ignorance. Also, I felt the truth of what he said; so I gave up listening, and amused myself by observing my new comrades. According to my classification of humanity, into persons "comme il faut" and persons not "comme il faut," they evidently belonged to the latter category, and so aroused in me not only a feeling of contempt, but also a certain sensation of personal hostility, for the reason that, though not "comme il faut," they accounted me their equal, and actually patronised me in a sort of good-humoured fashion. What in particular excited in me this feeling was their feet, their dirty nails and fingers, a particularly long talon on Operoff's obtrusive little finger, their red shirts, their dickeys, the chaff which they good-naturedly threw at one another, the dirty room, a habit which Zuchin had of continually snuffling and pressing a finger to his nose, and, above all, their manner of speaking—that is to say, their use and intonation of words. For instance, they said "flat" for fool, "just the ticket" for exactly, "grandly" for splendidly, and so on—all of which seemed to me either bookish or disagreeably vulgar. Still more was my "comme il faut" refinement disturbed by the accents which they put upon certain Russian—and, still more, upon foreign—words. Thus they said dieYATelnost for DIEyatelnost, NARochno for naROChno, v'KAMinie for v'kaMINie, SHAKespeare for ShakesPEARe, and so forth.

Yet, for all their insuperably repellent exterior, I could detect something good in these fellows, and envied them the cheerful good-fellowship which united them in one. Consequently, I began to feel attracted towards them, and made up my mind that, come what might, I would become of their number. The kind and honourable Operoff I knew already, and now the brusque, but exceptionally clever, Zuchin (who evidently took the lead in this circle) began to please me greatly. He was a dark, thick-set little fellow, with a perennially glistening, polished face, but one that was extremely lively, intellectual, and independent in its expression. That expression it derived from a low, but prominent, forehead, deep black eyes, short, bristly hair, and a thick, dark beard which looked as though it stood in constant need of trimming. Although, too, he seemed to think nothing of himself (a trail which always pleased me in people), it was clear that he never let his brain rest. He had one of those expressive faces which, a few hours after you have seen them for the first time, change suddenly and entirely to your view. Such a change took place, in my eyes, with regard to Zuchin's face towards the end of that evening. Suddenly, I seemed to see new wrinkles appear upon its surface, its eyes grow deeper, its smile become a different one, and the whole face assume such an altered aspect that I scarcely recognised it.

When the reading was ended, Zuchin, the other students, and myself manifested our desire to be "comrades all" by drinking vodka until little remained in the bottle. Thereupon Zuchin asked if any one had a quarter-rouble to spare, so that he could send the old woman who looked after him to buy some more; yet, on my offering to provide the money, he made as though he had not heard me, and turned to Operoff, who pulled out a purse sewn with bugles, and handed him the sum required.

"And mind you don't get drunk," added the giver, who himself had not partaken of the vodka.

"By heavens!" answered Zuchin as he sucked the marrow out of a mutton bone (I remember thinking that it must be because he ate marrow that he was so clever). "By heavens!" he went on with a slight smile (and his smile was of the kind that one involuntarily noticed, and somehow felt grateful for), "even if I did get drunk, there would be no great harm done. I wonder which of us two could look after himself the better—you or I? Anyway I am willing to make the experiment," and he slapped his forehead with mock boastfulness. "But what a pity it is that Semenoff has disappeared! He has gone and completely hidden himself somewhere."

Sure enough, the grey-haired Semenoff who had comforted me so much at my first examination by being worse dressed than myself, and who, after passing the second examination, had attended his lectures regularly during the first month, had disappeared thereafter from view, and never been seen at the University throughout the latter part of the course.

"Where is he?" asked some one.

"I do not know" replied Zuchin. "He has escaped my eye altogether. Yet what fun I used to have with him! What fire there was in the man! and what an intellect! I should be indeed sorry if he has come to grief—and come to grief he probably has, for he was no mere boy to take his University course in instalments."

After a little further conversation, and agreeing to meet again the next night at Zuchin's, since his abode was the most central point for us all, we began to disperse. As, one by one, we left the room, my conscience started pricking me because every one seemed to be going home on foot, whereas I had my drozhki. Accordingly, with some hesitation I offered Operoff a lift. Zuchin came to the door with us, and, after borrowing a rouble of Operoff, went off to make a night of it with some friends. As we drove along, Operoff told me a good deal about Zuchin's character and mode of life, and on reaching home it was long before I could get to sleep for thinking of the new acquaintances I had made. For many an hour, as I lay awake, I kept wavering between the respect which their knowledge, simplicity, and sense of honour, as well as the poetry of their youth and courage, excited in my regard, and the distaste which I felt for their outward man. In spite of my desire to do so, it was at that time literally impossible for me to associate with them, since our ideas were too wholly at variance. For me, life's meaning and charm contained an infinitude of shades of which they had not an inkling, and vice versa. The greatest obstacles of all, however, to our better acquaintance I felt to be the twenty roubles' worth of cloth in my tunic, my drozhki, and my white linen shirt; and they appeared to me most important obstacles, since they made me feel as though I had unwittingly insulted these comrades by displaying such tokens of my wealth. I felt guilty in their eyes, and as though, whether I accepted or rejected their acquittal and took a line of my own, I could never enter into equal and unaffected relations with them. Yet to such an extent did the stirring poetry of the courage which I could detect in Zuchin (in particular) overshadow the coarse, vicious side of his nature that the latter made no unpleasant impression upon me.

For a couple of weeks I visited Zuchin's almost every night for purposes of work. Yet I did very little there, since, as I have said, I had lost ground at the start, and, not having sufficient grit in me to catch up my companions by solitary study, was forced merely to PRETEND that I was listening to and taking in all they were reading. I have an idea, too, that they divined my pretence, since I often noticed that they passed over points which they themselves knew without first inquiring of me whether I did the same. Yet, day by day, I was coming to regard the vulgarity of this circle with more indulgence, to feel increasingly drawn towards its way of life, and to find in it much that was poetical. Only my word of honour to Dimitri that I would never indulge in dissipation with these new comrades kept me from deciding also to share their diversions.

Once, I thought I would make a display of my knowledge of literature, particularly French literature, and so led the conversation to that theme. Judge, then, of my surprise when I discovered that not only had my companions been reading the foreign passages in Russian, but that they had studied far more foreign works than I had, and knew and could appraise English, and even Spanish, writers of whom I had never so much as heard! Likewise, Pushkin and Zhukovski represented to them LITERATURE, and not, as to myself, certain books in yellow covers which I had once read and studied when a child. For Dumas and Sue they had an almost equal contempt, and, in general, were competent to form much better and clearer judgments on literary matters than I was, for all that I refused to recognise the fact. In knowledge of music, too, I could not beat them, and was astonished to find that Operoff played the violin, and another student the cello and piano, while both of them were members of the University orchestra, and possessed a wide knowledge of and appreciation of good music. In short, with the exception of the French and German languages, my companions were better posted at every point than I was, yet not the least proud of the fact. True, I might have plumed myself on my position as a man of the world, but Woloda excelled me even in that. Wherein, then, lay the height from which I presumed to look down upon these comrades? In my acquaintanceship with Prince Ivan Ivanovitch? In my ability to speak French? In my drozhki? In my linen shirt? In my finger-nails? "Surely these things are all rubbish," was the thought which would come flitting through my head under the influence of the envy which the good-fellowship and kindly, youthful gaiety displayed around me excited in my breast. Every one addressed his interlocutor in the second person singular. True, the familiarity of this address almost approximated to rudeness, yet even the boorish exterior of the speaker could not conceal a constant endeavour never to hurt another one's feelings. The terms "brute" or "swine," when used in this good-natured fashion, only convulsed me, and gave me cause for inward merriment. In no way did they offend the person addressed, or prevent the company at large from remaining on the most sincere and friendly footing. In all their intercourse these youths were delicate and forbearing in a way that only very poor and very young men can be. However much I might detect in Zuchin's character and amusements an element of coarseness and profligacy, I could also detect the fact that his drinking-bouts were of a very different order to the puerility with burnt rum and champagne in which I had participated at Baron Z.'s.

XLIV

ZUCHIN AND SEMENOFF

Although I do not know what class of society Zuchin belonged to, I know that, without the help either of means or social position, he had matriculated from the Seventh Gymnasium. At that time he was eighteen—though he looked much older—and very clever, especially in his powers of assimilation. To him it was easier to survey the whole of some complicated subject, to foresee its various parts and deductions, than to use that knowledge, when gained, for reasoning out the exact laws to which those deductions were due. He knew that he was clever, and of the fact he was proud; yet from that very pride arose the circumstance that he treated every one with unvarying simplicity and good-nature. Moreover, his experience of life must have been considerable, for already he had squandered much love, friendship, activity, and money. Though poor and moving only in the lower ranks of society, there was nothing which he had ever attempted for which he did not thenceforth feel the contempt, the indifference, or the utter disregard which were bound to result from his attaining his goal too easily. In fact, the very ardour with which he applied himself to a new pursuit seemed to be due to his contempt for what he had already attained, since his abilities always led him to success, and therefore to a certain right to despise it. With the sciences it was the same. Though little interested in them, and taking no notes, he knew mathematics thoroughly, and was uttering no vain boast when he said that he could beat the professor himself. Much of what he heard said in lectures he thought rubbish, yet with his peculiar habit of unconsciously practical roguishness he feigned to subscribe to all that the professors thought important, and every professor adored him. True, he was outspoken to the authorities, but they none the less respected him. Besides disliking and despising the sciences, he despised all who laboured to attain what he himself had mastered so easily, since the sciences, as he understood them, did not occupy one-tenth part of his powers. In fact, life, as he saw it from the student's standpoint, contained nothing to which he could devote himself wholly, and his impetuous, active nature (as he himself often said) demanded life complete: wherefore he frequented the drinking-bout in so far as he could afford it, and surrendered himself to dissipation chiefly out of a desire to get as far away from himself as possible. Consequently, just as the examinations were approaching, Operoff's prophecy to me came true, for Zuchin wasted two whole weeks in this fashion, and we had to do the latter part of our preparation at another student's. Yet at the first examination he reappeared with pale, haggard face and tremulous hands, and passed brilliantly into the second course!

The company of roisterers of which Zuchin had been the leader since its formation at the beginning of the term consisted of eight students, among whom, at first, had been numbered Ikonin and Semenoff; but the former had left under the strain of the continuous revelry in which the band had indulged in the early part of the term, and the latter seceded later for reasons which were never wholly explained. In its early days this band had been looked upon with awe by all the fellows of our course, and had had its exploits much discussed. Of these exploits the leading heroes had been Zuchin and, towards the end of the term, Semenoff, but the latter had come to be generally shunned, and to cause disturbances on the rare occasions when he attended a lecture. Just before the examinations began, he rounded off his drinking exploits in a most energetic and original fashion, as I myself had occasion to witness (through my acquaintanceship with Zuchin). This is how it was. One evening we had just assembled at Zuchin's, and Operoff, reinforcing a candlestick with a candle stuck in a bottle, had just plunged his nose into his notebooks and begun to read aloud in his thin voice from his neatly-written notes on physics, when the landlady entered the room, and informed Zuchin that some one had brought a note for him. . . (The remainder of this chapter is omitted in the original.)

XLV

I Come to Grief

At length the first examination—on differentials and integrals—drew near, but I continued in a vague state which precluded me from forming any clear idea of what was awaiting me. Every evening, after consorting with Zuchin and the rest, the thought would occur to me that there was something in my convictions which I must change—something wrong and mistaken; yet every morning the daylight would find me again satisfied to be "comme il faut," and desirous of no change whatsoever.

Such was the frame of mind in which I attended for the first examination. I seated myself on the bench where the princes, counts, and barons always sat, and began talking to them in French, with the not unnatural result that I never gave another thought to the answers which I was shortly to return to questions in a subject of which I knew nothing. I gazed supinely at other students as they went up to be examined, and even allowed myself to chaff some of them.

"Well, Grap," I said to Ilinka (who, from our first entry into the University, had shaken off my influence, had ceased to smile when I spoke to him, and always remained ill-disposed towards me), "have you survived the ordeal?"

"Yes," retorted Ilinka. "Let us see if You can do so."

I smiled contemptuously at the answer, notwithstanding that the doubt which he had expressed had given me a momentary shock. Once again, however, indifference overlaid that feeling, and I remained so entirely absent-minded and supine that, the very moment after I had been examined (a mere formality for me, as it turned out) I was making a dinner appointment with Baron Z. When called out with Ikonin, I smoothed the creases in my uniform, and walked up to the examiner's table with perfect sang froid.

True, a slight shiver of apprehension ran down my back when the young professor—the same one as had examined me for my matriculation—looked me straight in the face as I reached across to the envelope containing the tickets. Ikonin, though taking a ticket with the same plunge of his whole body as he had done at the previous examinations, did at least return some sort of an answer this time, though a poor one. I, on the contrary, did just as he had done on the two previous occasions, or even worse, since I took a second ticket, yet for a second time returned no answer. The professor looked me compassionately in the face, and said in a quiet, but determined, voice:

"You will not pass into the second course, Monsieur Irtenieff. You had better not complete the examinations. The faculty must be weeded out. The same with you, Monsieur Ikonin."

Ikonin implored leave to finish the examinations, as a great favour, but the professor replied that he (Ikonin) was not likely to do in two days what he had not succeeded in doing in a year, and that he had not the smallest chance of passing. Ikonin renewed his humble, piteous appeals, but the professor was inexorable.

"You can go, gentlemen," he remarked in the same quiet, resolute voice.

I was only too glad to do so, for I felt ashamed of seeming, by my silent presence, to be joining in Ikonin's humiliating prayers for grace. I have no recollection of how I threaded my way through the students in the hall, nor of what I replied to their questions, nor of how I passed into the vestibule and departed home. I was offended, humiliated, and genuinely unhappy.

For three days I never left my room, and saw no one, but found relief in copious tears. I should have sought a pistol to shoot myself if I had had the necessary determination for the deed. I thought that Ilinka Grap would spit in my face when he next met me, and that he would have the right to do so; that Operoff would rejoice at my misfortune, and tell every one of it; that Kolpikoff had justly shamed me that night at the restaurant; that my stupid speeches to Princess Kornikoff had had their fitting result; and so on, and so on. All the moments in my life which had been for me most difficult and painful recurred to my mind. I tried to blame some one for my calamity, and thought that some one must have done it on purpose—must have conspired a whole intrigue against me. Next, I murmured against the professors, against my comrades, Woloda, Dimitri, and Papa (the last for having sent me to the University at all). Finally, I railed at Providence for ever having let me see such ignominy. Believing myself ruined for ever in the eyes of all who knew me, I besought Papa to let me go into the hussars or to the Caucasus. Naturally, Papa was anything but pleased at what had happened; yet, on seeing my passionate grief, he comforted me by saying that, though it was a bad business, it might yet be mended by my transferring to another faculty. Woloda, who also saw nothing very terrible in my misfortune, added that at least I should not be put out of countenance in a new faculty, since I should have new comrades there. As for the ladies of the household, they neither knew nor cared what either an examination or a plucking meant, and condoled with me only because they saw me in such distress. Dimitri came to see me every day, and was very kind and consolatory throughout; but for that very reason he seemed to me to have grown colder than before. It always hurt me and made me feel uncomfortable when he came up to my room and seated himself in silence beside me, much as a doctor might scat himself by the bedside of an awkward patient. Sophia Ivanovna and Varenika sent me books for which I had expressed a wish, as also an invitation to go and see them, but in that very thoughtfulness of theirs I saw only proud, humiliating condescension to one who had fallen beyond forgiveness. Although, in three days' time, I grew calmer, it was not until we departed for the country that I left the house, but spent the time in nursing my grief and wandering, fearful of all the household, through the various rooms.

One evening, as I was sitting deep in thought and listening to Avdotia playing her waltz, I suddenly leapt to my feet, ran upstairs, got out the copy-book whereon I had once inscribed "Rules of My Life," opened it, and experienced my first moment of repentance and moral resolution. True, I burst into tears once more, but they were no longer tears of despair. Pulling myself together, I set about writing out a fresh set of rules, in the assured conviction that never again would I do a wrong action, waste a single moment on frivolity, or alter the rules which I now decided to frame.

How long that moral impulse lasted, what it consisted of, and what new principles I devised for my moral growth I will relate when speaking of the ensuing and happier portion of my early manhood.

A Note About the Author

Leo Tolstoy (1828–1910) was a Russian author of novels, short stories, novellas, plays, and philosophical essays. He was born into an aristocratic family and served as an officer in the Russian military during the Crimean War before embarking on a career as a writer and activist. Tolstoy's experience in war, combined with his interpretation of the teachings of Jesus, led him to devote his life and work to the cause of pacifism. In addition to such fictional works as *War and Peace* (1869), *Anna Karenina* (1877), and *The Death of Ivan Ilyich* (1886), Tolstoy wrote *The Kingdom of God is Within You* (1893), a philosophical treatise on nonviolent resistance which had a profound impact on Mahatma Gandhi and Martin Luther King Jr. He is regarded today not only as one of the greatest writers of all time, but as a gifted and passionate political figure and public intellectual whose work transcends Russian history and literature alike.

A Note from the Publisher

Spanning many genres, from non-fiction essays to literature classics to children's books and lyric poetry, Mint Edition books showcase the master works of our time in a modern new package. The text is freshly typeset, is clean and easy to read, and features a new note about the author in each volume. Many books also include exclusive new introductory material. Every book boasts a striking new cover, which makes it as appropriate for collecting as it is for gift giving. Mint Edition books are only printed when a reader orders them, so natural resources are not wasted. We're proud that our books are never manufactured in excess and exist only in the exact quantity they need to be read and enjoyed.

Discover more of your favorite classics with Bookfinity™.

- Track your reading with custom book lists.
- Get great book recommendations for your personalized Reader Type.
- Add reviews for your favorite books.
- AND MUCH MORE!

Visit **bookfinity.com** and take the fun Reader Type quiz to get started.

Enjoy our classic and modern companion pairings!

Classic & Modern